AN UNDETERMINED MANNER OF DEATH

An Undetermined Manner of Death

medical noir fiction

by PETER TINITS MD

Dying Medium Press

Copyright © Peter Tinits, 2023

All rights reserved. No part of this book may be used or reproduced in any manner without prior written permission of the author, except in the use of brief quotations embodied in reviews.

This book is a work of fiction. Names, characters, incidents and the cities of Coventry and Somerset, Ontario are products of the author's imagination. Any resemblance to actual persons, living or dead, or to actual events or locales is entirely coincidental. The cities of Pickering and Toronto do in fact exist.

Name: Tinits, Peter, author

Title: *An UNDETERMINED MANNER of DEATH*

Description: The attractive beneficiary of a new life insurance policy promotes a homicide verdict to the coroner investigating her father's apparent suicide.

Subject: fiction/medical, crime, mystery and detective

BISAC: FIC 035000, FIC050000, FIC022020

ISBN: 978-1-7771904-5-3 (softcover), 978-1-7771904-6-0 (EPUB)

Cover art by Stan Oshima
Operating room illustration by Scott O'Neill
Cover design by Ted Glaszewski

Thanks to my second-best beta reader Andrus Voitk

Reality is for people who can't face drugs —Tom Waits

I don't need drugs to make my life tragic —Eddie Vedder

Well, whatever, nevermind —Kurt Cobain

Chapter 1

The right rear tire on my sport utility vehicle had looked flattish in the morning. Loving the planet doesn't preclude loving four-wheel drive and survivalist tire tread. I drove to work at the hospital on it anyway because I was late, and had just driven back home on it holding my breath. My handicap is not being handy. The Canadian Automobile Association would have to come put on the spare.

Because Friday is followed by Saturday, it could wait until tomorrow. I was going to a TGIF get-together across town. Living in Coventry, a city of 50,000 inhabitants, meant nothing was too far to be reached by bicycle. I began cycling year round to maintain my bliss when Covid closed the gyms.

Twenty minutes later, I was fastening my bike to a yield sign with the giant U-shaped kryptonite lock that I carried on the frame. It was probably safe enough at a cop retirement party. Following the sound of talking and laughing, I wandered alongside the house to the back yard.

There were 30 or 40 people standing in groups, whom I judged to be either cops or neighbours. I was considering which group to attach myself to when one of the cops called, "Hey Matt." He came over holding a beer and extending one.

"Hey Jackson. Congratulations on your retirement!" I said.

"Thanks man. I'm free for alternative employment now—I was thinking you could use a chauffeur."

"Did you see me arrive on my bike?"

"No. I mean to drive you around on your coroner job. It would be the perfect retirement job for me."

"There's no budget for that. You know I only do one or two coroner calls per month, right? I'm still working as an anesthesiologist."

Jackson looked disappointed. "Well, let me know if business picks up. Driving with lights and sirens is my only real, marketable skill."

Detective Branko Marcovic emerged from the side of the house and approached, wearing a tie and an ethnic-looking sweater-vest. He was tall and thin with a hook nose that looked like it had been broken and left to heal.

"Hey Branko. Thanks for coming," Jackson said.

"I'm supposed to be working, but I couldn't very well miss your special day, could I Jackson. I see you followed my advice."

"What was that?" I asked.

Branko coughed. "In your last week at work, don't shoot anyone and don't get shot."

"They wouldn't let me take any calls for the week before I retired," Jackson confided.

"Hey Matt. We had a guy hanging from a tree yesterday. Couldn't find a coroner," Branko said.

"Yeah, they called me at work," I said. "I couldn't go. Is he still there?"

"No. He'd been there since midnight yesterday though. Pierce said it was a psychiatric patient who suicided." Pierce was the other coroner in town. "We also had a good case last month of a corpse holding his severed penis in his left hand. What do you think of that, Matt?"

"I would say he was right-handed, unless his wife cut it off."

"The wife said she didn't do it," Branko said, deadpan. "She was too fond of it."

"That's reassuring," I said.

"She also said she couldn't have done it because it was hard as nails," Jackson said, "but I noticed she had a chipped tooth."

"Did he really bleed out from that?" I asked.

"No," Branko said. "He took a lot of pills also."

"See, that's two good cases you missed by being an anesthesiologist, Matt," Jackson said. "You should do coronering full time and then you *would* need a driver. Get yourselves beer and munchies from the picnic table. I have to circulate." He wandered off.

"Nice sweater," I said, looking for something to say. Branko normally wore a cheap baggy suit. Detectives need the extra fabric to conceal their guns.

"Thanks."

"I'm wearing a nice shirt. You forgot to mention it."

Branko smiled. "How are relations with the surgeons these days?"

"Good. We have an understanding. You know that song, 'Fuck you, I won't do what you tell me'?"

"Yeah, it's a good song. It doesn't work that way in my world," Branko said.

"Mine either, really."

I stayed until it got dark and then went back to the curb to get my bicycle. Taking the scenic route home, I entered the park where there was a bike path that was lit up at night. As I was climbing a steep hill, the chain started slipping over the teeth of the front sprocket. The chain had rusted from winter road salt and needed to be replaced. Pushing the bike the rest of the way up the hill, I heard the sound of two men arguing.

Their voices quietened as I approached. One of the men seemed to be twice the age of the other. They were both scrawny and in need of a shower. The older one turned away from me as I passed, but one eye still saw me. His eyes were looking in divergent directions. The strabismus and his anger made him look crazy. Not wanting to provoke comments, I went by quickly.

Off in the distance, I heard, "No!"

"Why not? Let's report seeing someone coming down a ladder."

"Shut your word-hole and stick to the fucking plan, fucktard."

"Why do you always have to turn into…"

I didn't hear the rest of it and didn't want to. They were probably arguing over drugs or the proceeds of a drug deal. I exited the park and cycled home on sidewalks to avoid cars and sewer grates that could kill me.

Chapter 2

My wife Katya peeked at me through half-closed eyelids as I moved around the bedroom. She had curled her five-foot-ten-inch length into a blanket-wrapped cocoon. She built up a sleep deficit during the week, marking papers and preparing lessons, that needed to be rectified. As a high school teacher, she was also stressed out from negotiating with teenagers. Her blonde-with-pink-fringes hairdo had bedhead, but she looked comfortable and happy.

"Sleeping late?" I asked.

"It's the weekend."

"You got over nine hours sleep last night."

"Nine is just a number. I like to get up when I'm ready."

"Doing anything today?"

"Returning empty wine bottles and visiting my sister."

Katya's twin sister Magda lived in Pickering, an hour's drive away. They talked or texted or visited nearly every day. They communicated in Polish when they didn't want me to understand.

"Why? Were they defective?"

"Ha. Ha." Katya stretched all four limbs like a snow angel.

"You should say they were empty when you bought them. You used to love your glass of wine before bed."

Katya couldn't tolerate any alcohol now. She said it made her nauseous. This might have subliminally had something to do with feature news items about alcohol being a carcinogen. I stepped over Madame Fifi, who was twitching and growling on the floor, to get to the closet.

"Do you think she is dreaming of electric sheep?" Katya asked.

"Most replicants do."

"What about you? What are you up to today?"

"I have to get my back tire fixed. One of my enemies slashed it."

Katya struggled out of bed and staggered toward the bathroom. She was wearing a T-shirt and terry-cloth shorts cinched with a drawstring, variations of which she generally always slept in. Katya is a bit ungainly, as if she didn't expect to grow as tall as she did. This little vulnerability is endearing.

"Okay hon, if you say so," she said.

"Okay hon, I'm just going out to take care of it." Hon was an epithet we used ironically because we were above plebeian endearments.

"Kisses, my bunny." Katya planted a kiss in passing that half missed my mouth.

Walking around my SUV in the driveway, I noticed that the back tire was now completely flat. I pulled the plasticized CAA card from my wallet and dialled their service number on my phone. As I was waiting on hold, I got an alert that there was a call from the coroner's answering service. They never chose to call at a convenient time. I hesitated and then swiped right.

There was a death at an apartment house in Coventry of a 58-year-old man, a Mr. Albert Yantzi, who was the lone occupant. They gave me his date of birth and the telephone number of a policeman at the scene. I called the number and heard, "Hi Doctor. We have a 58-year-old male, found dead by his landlord on the floor of his apartment. The fire department is waiting for you."

"What do you mean 'the fire department is waiting for me'?"

"You'll see when you get here."

"That's it? Is there any evidence of trauma? Are there any pill bottles around?"

"It's hard to know. It's better if you see for yourself." He gave me directions and hung up.

Searching Albert Yantzi quickly on the Coventry Hospital computer database brought up one emergency department visit for a twisted ankle. There was no family doctor. He was either previously healthy, had received his medical care somewhere else or was a derelict who avoided doctors and hospitals. I copied down the phone number for a daughter who was next of kin.

Slinging my coroner bag over my shoulder, I cycled ten minutes to the scene. There were two fire engines and three police cars parked by the side of the road in front of a six-plex apartment house. Several firemen in brown jumpsuits and five or six policemen were milling around. Cops will often congregate and just hang out if it's a slow day and something interesting or unusual has happened. One of the cops approached, and I handed him my business card.

"I've already got one, Dr. Kork"

I'm bad with names and faces. "Could I have one of yours?"

He extended a card from his wallet that bore the name Hunter Schultz, Constable, Coventry Police. "The firemen will get you suited up in a hazmat suit."

"Why? What's going on? Are you the investigating officer?"

"That would be Branko Marcovic. He'll escort you in. I'm the one you spoke with on the phone. We've opened up all the windows, but it's still pretty overwhelming. The firemen have to leave soon."

"When was this guy last seen alive?"

"His girlfriend came to visit, noticed the smell and notified the superintendent. He called us and unlocked the door. The last person to see Albert alive was the same girlfriend three weeks ago."

Hunter escorted me to a firetruck where there was a pile of equipment on the ground. The firemen fitted me into a plastic zip-up hazmat suit with a shroud covering my head. They threaded my arms through the harness of a scuba tank that sat on my back and pulled on my shoulders. I put on my own disposable gloves.

"That too heavy for you, Doc?"

"No. Is this mouthpiece clean?"

"Yeah, well, we wiped it off. Put it in your mouth to test it out. You've got about half a tank. Try to breathe at a slow even rate so you don't use up the air supply too quickly. If your air is low, you'll hear an alarm. Okay? Come this way then."

They led me to the building entrance where Branko was speaking with another officer. He was wearing the same gear as me.

"Hi Matt. I've got his health card for you here—a Mr. Albert Yantzi. You can use the photo to make the identification."

"How come so many cops are here, Branko?"

"Albert is lying beside a long gun. It doesn't look like it's been discharged though."

"Yantzi is a Mennonite name. It's weird for a Mennonite to be living in the city alone."

"He might have been excommunicated," Branko suggested.

"Any drugs in the apartment that he could have overdosed on?"

"Maybe. It's a pigsty in there. We did find a few prescription drug bottles for you to look at."

Branko put his mouthpiece in and motioned for me to do the same. We ascended a flight of stairs through sequential waves of flies in their thousands arriving at plate glass windows in the stairwell. The windows acted like magnifying glasses to concentrate the heat of the noon-day sun. As we entered the second-floor apartment, the stench of decay was disgusting despite our air tanks.

The living room was dishevelled, with scattered clothes and garbage littering the floor and every level surface. There were two cops, one of them with a camera taking pictures. A balcony door was wide open. The decedent was lying on his back with his arms at his sides and his head turned to the left on the living-room floor beside an unmade pull-out bed.

His face was a bloated, black beachball surrounded by a cloud of flies. Maggots wriggled in his right eye. His left eye seemed to be eaten away or missing. There was a circular pool of congealed blood or bloody vomit on the floor around his head. Blood propelled by gas escaping from a decomposing stomach can do this. His body was a mottled blue-green. His fingers were shrivelled to bony remnants. A rusty, vintage Winchester-style rifle was lying by his side on the floor, exactly parallel to the body.

I took my mouthpiece out long enough to say, "You don't think he shot himself?"

Branko took his mouthpiece out long enough to say, "I don't think it's been fired."

Removing my mouthpiece again, "What about his left eye?"

"That's not an entry wound."

Branko held the decedent's provincial health insurance card photo beside his head for me to look at. I peered at it intensely and then at the dead man's face, and then back and forth. It was hard to be sure. I probed his lips with my index finger to see if he had teeth, but they were swollen shut and I didn't want to get cut.

There was no visible bullet hole in the front of his T-shirt or jeans. I didn't attempt to turn or undress him as his skin was slippery and lifting off in sheets. They would do that during the autopsy anyway. He was wearing socks but no shoes. I took off the left sock and forced it over the distended right one so it wouldn't get lost. To his bare big toe, I attached the toe tag that I had completed with a Sharpie marker at home with the name that dispatch had given me.

The kitchen counter was crowded with take-out wrappers and dirty dishes encrusted with dried and decaying food. The refrigerator held a case of beer, two bottles of cola, a bowl of what might have been hamburger meat and a box of baking soda. There were two neatly stacked crates of empty beer cans in the cupboard. I went into the bathroom and it was filthy too. There was an actual layer of grime on the counter under the empty cardboard packages and vitamin bottles.

That was it—three rooms in total. They could put the *Vacancy, Nice Studio Apartment* sign out on the lawn. Branko had grouped prescription bottles together for me on the corner of a living-room end table where he had pushed beer cans to one side to clear a spot. The ancient labels were faded and almost illegible. There was an antihypertensive, an antidepressant and a proton pump inhibitor to decrease stomach acidity, all prescribed by a family doctor whom I knew to be retired. I didn't see any illicit drugs or drug paraphernalia.

As I was reading the labels, my low air alarm went off. Branko heard it as well. Casting another look around the apartment, I exited past the hot swarms of flies in the stairwell as expeditiously as my dignity would allow. Branko followed in my wake.

When we got outside, Branko said, "I think you possibly inhaled some fly poop. How long do you think he's been dead?"

"Maybe four weeks, maybe as little as two or three, depending on how hot it got in the apartment. I've never seen anyone that decomposed before."

"We were leaving the rifle in place until the ident team from Toronto finished with photos and you had a chance to look at the layout. They'll take the rifle for fingerprinting. I got the distance from the end of the barrel to the trigger at nine and a half inches."

I got his meaning. "I'll tell the pathologist to measure his arm length to see if he could have reached the trigger. Was that balcony door locked when they found him?"

"Closed, but not locked. The front door to the apartment was locked."

"How did the flies get in? Could you ID him from that health card photo, Branko?"

"Yes."

"Are you sure?"

"Pretty sure. Who else would it be?"

"It's strange that the rifle is lying exactly parallel to the body."

"Like a soldier. That's why I don't think he used it. There was no ammunition around anywhere. There is a bracket on the wall where the rifle might have been mounted as a decoration."

"He might have been considering using it and took some pills instead," I said. "Did you see the beer cans in the kitchen cupboard. He was planning to return the empties for a refund."

Branko smiled. "Ten cents each."

"I noticed a video camera in the lobby."

"The super thinks it's broken. Most residential cameras only store security footage for a week or two before it's overwritten, but we'll look into it."

"Were you able to find a next of kin?" Speaking with next of kin is stressed in coroners' training. The coroners' office is very conscious of public relations.

"He has an estranged daughter who lives out of town. She hasn't seen him in ten years."

"Have you spoken with her?"

Branko flipped through his notebook for her number. "We talked to her on the phone. She was pretty cold about the whole thing."

As this was more complex than the usual case, I called the Regional Supervising Coroner on call for advice. It was Richard Tull, who also happened to be my regular supervisor. I told him my findings and, as I was wrapping up, he asked whether I was able to make a positive identification.

"Well, it's presumptive. He *is* decomposed. His head is bloated and black."

"Does he have teeth? Does he have any tattoos?"

"I don't know about tattoos. There is skin slippage, so I couldn't undress him without bullae lifting off in sheets. He may have some teeth left. His face is edematous and his lips are sort of sealed together." I didn't say I had been afraid of cutting myself by pushing my finger too far into his mouth.

"Do the police have any fingerprints on file for him?"

"I'll find out, but I don't think he has any fingerprints left."

"Did you get a toothbrush or hairbrush for DNA analysis?"

"No."

"Well, you'll have to go back and get one of those."

I had a look over at where the firemen had parked. They were packing away the last of their equipment. A moment later, they got into their trucks and drove away.

"Okay," I said. "I'll have another look around his bathroom." Good soldiers *can do*.

I was standing beside Hunter Schultz again. I told him I needed a toothbrush or hairbrush and then walked back toward the building without waiting for him to offer. Taking a last giant lung-full of fresh air, I mounted the stairs and re-entered the apartment. The smell wasn't so bad once you got used to it.

I waded back through the trash to the bathroom. After some digging, I found a fuzzy hairbrush and worn toothbrush on the counter and shoved them together into a plastic bag. Without further ado, I left the apartment for the second time and found Branko.

"Okay, you can call the body removal service—Christobel's or Schade's Funeral Home—whichever you like. I think Christobel's might be quicker."

Funeral homes do body removals for autopsies as a sideline. They compete with each other for the business. To avoid being accused of playing favourites, I let the police decide.

"Already done," he replied.

"And send these with the body," I handed him the plastic bag. "Does he have a criminal record? Are there any fingerprints on file?"

"No. Do you want us to hold the scene?"

"Not for my purposes."

"Okay. We'll preserve it long enough to look for spent rifle casings. Be nice to your wife so you don't end up alone, decomposing for two to four weeks."

"I have to call the pathologist now to tell him that I'm sending him a body," I said. "They're going to ask me whether you want to attend the autopsy."

"Not really…" His face showed veiled disgust. "Okay. Tell them yes."

The on-call forensic pathologist in Toronto was Dr. Ron Rasmussen. Forensic pathologists consider themselves higher up the food chain than coroners. I'd spoken with him a few times in the past.

I got him on the phone. "Hi. This is Dr. Matthew Kork. I'm a coroner in Coventry."

"Yes, I know. Hi."

"I'm sending you a badly decomposed body, a Mr. Albert Yantzi, whom I have tentatively identified. He was in his locked apartment. The superintendent called it in because of the smell. He was last seen alive by a girlfriend approximately three weeks ago. It may have been a natural death or a drug overdose. He is supine on the floor with some blood or bloody purge around his head. There is a vintage rifle by his side that doesn't appear to have been fired."

"How are we going to identify him?"

"I had a look at his health card photo, but I can't be sure."

"So, how are you going to identify him?" He wanted it to be my problem.

"I'm sending you a hair and toothbrush for DNA. There is a daughter who is next of kin, but she's estranged. I'll ask her if he had a dentist when I speak with her. The medical records don't give a history of any joint implants."

"Does he have teeth?"

"I'm not sure. His lips are swollen shut."

"Okay. Ask her about tattoos. Do the police want to attend?"

"Yes."

"Tell them 8 a.m. tomorrow. I'll call you tomorrow." He hung up.

When I got home, I stripped down to my underwear, leaving my clothes by the door, and went directly to shower. I hadn't decided whether to wash or burn the clothes.

Chapter 3

The automobile association tow truck came to my house in the afternoon and the driver substituted my spare tire for the flat. The driver liked the FJ Cruiser so much that he told me to call him whenever I was ready to sell. The vehicle had a distinctive appearance and had developed a cult following since Toyota ceased making that model. He actually thanked me for taking good care of it.

I called River Auto Service to see if they would patch the punctured tire. The owner, Derek, and I were friendly. The Province of Ontario used to require bi-annual vehicle exhaust emissions testing for older vehicles to renew their licence plates. As a favour, Derek had turned off the warning, check-engine light on the dashboard of my old truck and instructed me to drive directly to the test centre at Canadian Tire before it came back on. Unfortunately, I turned the motor off to go inside. As soon as they switched on the ignition for the test, the light came back.

Five hundred dollars later, they hadn't found why the light was on. As this was the maximum the province required any driver to pay for a diagnostic workup, I was free to drive it with the warning light illuminated for another year. Anticipating that things would be no different in a year, I gave the truck to my sister and bought a new one. Derek told me I could bring my vehicle in an hour.

"I found a roofer's nail embedded to the hilt in your back tire," Derek said after patching the tire. "I mounted it on the back hatch so you can use it as a spare. Have you had your roof repaired recently?"

"Maybe about ten years ago."

"Well, sometimes there's a nail on the road that your front tire spins up so that it's exactly primed to hit your back tire. Your SUV also looks like it's been keyed on the passenger side."

"What! Where?"

"Over here," he said, indicating a scratch on the passenger door. "Got any enemies?"

"None that I know of. A few surgeons."

"Maybe the nail and the key job happened together. It could have been done with the same nail. If it's vandalism, your insurance would cover it."

"I guess it could be high school students. My wife says some of hers are criminals."

"If you balance the nail in this deep tread when the truck is parked, it will puncture the tire when the vehicle reverses to leave. You'll get a slow leak."

"Good to know."

"Still enjoying your SUV?" Derek inquired conspiratorially.

"Yes. I need the four-wheel drive for work in winter. It has stick shift like a racing car."

"Ever think of selling it?"

"No. I've had some interest."

"What do they call that colour? Tan?"

"It's called Quicksand."

"The guys in the shop were admiring it. They all said they would trade their own vehicles for it in a heartbeat."

Driving home, I was replaying recent movements in my mind to remember whether I had left the SUV somewhere it could have been vandalized. It could have happened anywhere. I had really only been to the shopping mall and hospital in the last few days. Katya had borrowed it once when she loaned her own car to our son Michael.

I put in a call to the estranged daughter in the evening. There was no answer, so I left my number on her voicemail. A review of the hospital medical records, which I could access from my home computer, showed that the decedent had had an inguinal hernia repair with mesh in 2001. He was on a cholesterol pill and an antidepressant, and he drank too much.

On Sunday morning, the pathologist, Dr. Rasmussen, called me from Toronto. He wasn't happy with the presumptive identification. Before starting the autopsy, he wanted to know whether the decedent had any joint replacements or metal plates or screws that would have shown up on old X-rays. He also wanted to know whether I had been able to find any old dental records. I told him no joint replacements. I was still trying to find out if he had a dentist.

"Well, get on it and let me know as soon as you can. We can also sometimes make the identification from the shape of the sinuses on a skull X-ray. Check if he ever had that."

"There isn't one in the databases that I checked. I sent you a hairbrush and a toothbrush for DNA analysis."

"We're holding onto those for now. What would matching them really prove? That takes a while anyway."

"Could you check his DNA against the daughter's?"

"Let's try the other things I mentioned first."

The estranged daughter, Taylor, called me back on Sunday afternoon. She sounded like she might be around 30-years-old. She told me she was sorry about not calling sooner, but that she had been traveling out of the country.

"Sorry for your loss," I said.

"Thank you."

"Are you coming to Coventry to attend to your father's affairs?" I asked.

"I haven't seen him in more than ten years. I don't know."

"I would like to ask you a few questions, Taylor. Do you have a few minutes?"

"Yes."

"Did your father drink or do drugs?"

"Yes. He drank a little. That was one of the reasons we didn't get along."

"What drugs did he do?"

"Just marijuana mainly, I think. He didn't do any hard drugs."

"Did he have any medical problems like heart disease or diabetes?"

"Maybe now—I don't know."

"Did he ever see a psychiatrist or talk about harming himself?"

"No, I don't think so. I don't know about the last ten years."

"He was prescribed antidepressants. Do you know anything about that?" This didn't mean much. Antidepressants are among the most commonly prescribed drugs in North America.

"No. I'm sorry."

"Okay Taylor, just to confirm his identification, did he have any tattoos? Has he had any joint replacements? Did he look after his teeth? Did he have a dentist?"

"We had a family dentist named Dr. Doyle about 20 years ago. I think he went there. He might have tattoos."

"Your father is having an autopsy later today. His body is at the Forensic Sciences Complex in Toronto. I'll call you with the preliminary result once I get it. Is this a good number to call you at?"

Taylor called me back an hour later and said she had decided to come to Coventry. I told her that if she went to her father's apartment to be prepared for a shock—that it was quite dishevelled. She said that she knew he wasn't a neat-freak. That was an understatement. I guess people become slovenly when they live alone and are alcoholics.

After a Google search, I found a Dr. Doyle whom I called on Monday morning from work at the hospital. A mature-sounding female receptionist looked up Albert Yantzi and said that he had been a patient. There had been no visit in the past 20 years. Records that old were stored off-site. I asked her when she would have time to check for old X-rays. She said not today. I was silent, as if that answer was unacceptable, waiting for a better one. After five seconds she said, possibly after the office closed. She would get back to me.

I only had a half-list in the O.R., so I went home for lunch. Katya was standing at the kitchen counter listening to the radio and chopping vegetables. She was making a salad of cucumbers, olives, tomatoes, onions, peppers and sliced avocado. She shook up her olive oil, vinegar, mustard, salt and pepper in a little jar, poured and settled.

"That looks healthy and delicious," I said.

"You want me to make you one?"

"It's all right."

I decided on a ham sandwich with a token doubled-up lettuce leaf between the slices of bread. She didn't look like she really wanted to get up. We officially only ate together at dinnertime.

"What was your coroner's case on Saturday?" Katya asked.

"A horribly decomposed body in an apartment. We had to go up in hazmat suits because of the flies and the smell. It was like a scene from Ghostbusters."

"Did he live alone?"

"Yes. If he had a husband or a wife, someone would have noticed he was dead."

"That's sad. What did he die of?"

"I'm not sure. He was supposed to have had an autopsy yesterday, but no one called me with the result. I don't think he suicided because he had neatly stacked his empty beer cans to return them for a refund. How was your visit with your sister?"

"Good."

"What did you do."

"We had lunch and went for a walk."

"Did you talk about me?"

"Of course."

"I don't like this America's-Got-Talent type whiny music," I said. "What stream are you listening to? Boo-hoo. Sing like a man."

"What *is* a man, Matt?" Katya asked.

"Big muscles, hairy chest, hairy prognathic chin, maybe some tats, big honkin' dick."

"That's it?"

"I think so."

"Big honkin' nose too," Katya said. "They go together."

I hoped she didn't know that from personal experience.

Pathologists are obliged to call coroners with the preliminary autopsy result on the day it is performed. I called Dr. Ron Rasmussen's number in Toronto after lunch and managed to get his secretary to put the call through.

"I was going to call you yesterday," he said, "but you put your number down as 1-2-3-4-5-6-7 on the Warrant for PM."

"Anything's possible, but I don't think so. It could have been auto-filled if I missed that field. My cell number was on the toe tag."

We had new online software for completing warrants and filing our reports that I wasn't used to yet. It auto-filled some fields but roughly doubled our workload with its census-like, administrators' wish-list of new blank fields to complete.

"Well, we were overwhelmed with work. I have some news for you. We passed him through a CT scanner, and found multiple bullet fragments in the left hemi-cranium."

"I was wondering whether he had shot himself in the left eye," I said, as if I wasn't completely surprised by this news.

"In the left ear. Directly into the left external auditory canal. The eye is not a site of election for self-inflicted wounds. Suicides prefer the heart, neck, temple or mouth."

"Sorry. I didn't notice that. I guess they don't want to see the shot coming."

I felt a little foolish. Mr. Yantzi was lying on his back with his head turned to the left. His head had been too slimy to turn.

"The brain was too decomposed to follow a tract. There was no exit wound. The bullet fragmented on the base of the skull. This was a low velocity bullet, but the increase in intracranial pressure from the shot seems to have caused his left eye to blow out. The orbital socket was empty. Do you know whether he was right or left-handed?"

"Sorry, I don't know about his handedness. I'll ask his daughter and see if she knows."

"He would be more likely to be left-handed if he suicided. There was some gunpowder stippling on the skin, so it was a medium range shot—from six inches to a foot away."

"Did you measure the length of his arms?" I asked.

"Yes, 41 inches. The police told me the distance from the tip of the barrel to the trigger was 29- and one-half inches. So, he could have reached the trigger."

"Okay thanks. What about his other organs?"

"He could also have engaged the trigger using one of his feet. He wasn't wearing shoes. The heart was too decomposed to make any findings. I dissected down to the spine. Did you say he had a hernia repair? I couldn't find any mesh."

Hernias were often closed by sewing polypropylene mesh into the abdominal wall defect.

"Yes. The surgical note from 2001 said that he had a large piece of mesh."

"Well, it might have been there. It doesn't show up on CT. I didn't find it. I'm not going back in." He obviously wanted to be rid of the malodourous liquid corpse.

"How did you cope with the smell doing the autopsy?" I asked. "It must have been awful."

"It wasn't that bad. I just wore an N-95 mask. Did you get the dental records?"

I wasn't sure if Ron was one-upping me with his tolerance for fetid odours. "I found a dental office that treated him 20 years ago. The records are in storage. The receptionist said she would check and get back to me. Did he have teeth?"

"He only had five left. Let me know about the dental records. We need to make a positive identification. There were no prosthetic joints or metal plates when we scanned him."

"What about DNA?"

"We're holding off for the time being. I'm releasing the body to the funeral home." Then, curtly, "Okay?" That meant the conversation was over.

"Just a thought—could you check his hands for gunshot residue? Would there still be some there if he suicided?"

"If there was any, it wouldn't be interpretable. From a medium range, it could be there if he discharged the weapon or if someone else did."

I emailed Branko to give him the preliminary autopsy result in case he hadn't attended. Then I called Taylor, the daughter, back to tell her the autopsy findings. She said she was just leaving to drive to Coventry to make arrangements with Christobel's Funeral Home.

I told her I was very sorry to have to say that her father had been shot in the head. It looked like a probable suicide. We were still waiting on toxicology and histology reports. That meant blood levels of drugs and microscopic tissue examination. The final coroner's report wouldn't be available until after these results were known. This might take several months. The time it took was beyond my control. She could apply in writing for a copy of the report.

Reviewing my notes as we talked, I saw that she had told me that her father hadn't seen a psychiatrist or had suicidal ideation, but she didn't know about the last ten years. I asked Taylor whether her father owned any firearms. She remembered that he had an old rifle, with a loop of metal behind the trigger, mounted on the wall and never used. Was he right or left-handed? She thought that he was left-handed. What about an inguinal hernia repair? She did seem to remember something like that.

Taylor dutifully transcribed the address to write for a copy of the final coroner's report as I dictated it to her. She could tell Christobel's Funeral Home that the body was now available for pick-up from the morgue in Toronto. Did she have any questions? She said no, thanked me and hung up.

Chapter 4

I was the anesthesiologist doing intravenous sedation for a list of 15 colonoscopies on Tuesday. Colonoscopy is a screening test for colon cancer. A surgeon threads a long black hose with a camera at the tip through the length of the colon examining the lining. Chandler Davis, a new, young general surgeon, was doing the scoping. He had inherited the time slot from Dr. Amodeo, who had joined the huddled masses yearning to breathe free and make some real coin in the United States of America.

Sara was in the colonoscopy suite as the circulating nurse. She was attractive—slim, age around 35, triangular feline face and large neon-green eyes. The three of us were dressed in operating room greens, but with optional mask or head covering since colonoscopy is not a sterile procedure. The terror, carnage and paranoia of three years of Covid was fading.

"Hi Chandler," Sara said. I thought I might have noticed her long eyelashes flutter.

"Hi," he said shyly. He didn't really know us yet.

"How are your children, Chandler? How old are they now?" Sara asked.

"I've got a baby and a two-year-old."

"Is the baby sleeping through the night yet?" I asked. Sleep was important to me.

"No, not yet."

"Are you getting up or your wife?" Sara asked.

"We take turns. My wife shares more of the burden to be honest."

"Your wife will get some time off when the older one is in school and the baby is in day care," Sara said.

"We're going to home-school them."

The first patient was a healthy 50-year-old woman. In the absence of other risk factors, fifty is the age when colonoscopic cancer screening often begins. This patient was also my real estate agent when I bought my house. She was Val Papadopolis of Papadopolis Realty. Val had a Jackie-Kennedy-bulbous-bouffant hairstyle and bright red lipstick despite the clear prohibition of makeup on the preoperative instruction sheet.

"I'm getting the VIP treatment," Val announced when she saw me approach. Her laugh was robust and brassy. "I think I know some nurses here too." That wasn't too uncommon in Coventry.

Sara and I brought her into the colonoscopy suite. We attached her to the monitors, put an oxygen mask on her face and settled her on her side with her backside exposed. The surgeon stood behind her poised and ready with the colonoscope in his hand. I told her I was giving her an intravenous benzodiazepine named midazolam to make her drowsy. I said I was starting with a lowish dose to judge the effect and remove her inhibitions.

Val was suggestible. Before my syringe had left the intravenous injection port, she boomed, "So, how would you rate my ass out of ten, Chandler?"

When he didn't answer, she repeated the question even more loudly.

"I don't know what you mean," Chandler finally said.

"My ass, Chandler, my ass! How would you rate it out of ten?" she insisted.

I got her deeper with more sedation until she was snoring.

"Okay, you can start," I said.

"Nobody cares about your ass," Chandler said.

"Every ass is beautiful in its own way, isn't it, Chandler?" Sara put a finger in her mouth and did a mock gag. "Been doing any coronering, Matt?"

"Some. My usual case is a death at home of an old person who lives alone. I spend 15 minutes looking up the history to determine that it's a natural death and 15 minutes trying to find a family doctor to look after it. Then, I spend 15 minutes doing the data entry. Since I haven't accepted the case for investigation, this pays me $30 total. If the body is decomposed, I have to take the case, which seems arbitrary."

"Were you called to that death in the six-plex down the street from me last Saturday?" Sara asked. "I know one of the people who lives there."

"Yeah, I had to go. Who do you know there?"

"A neighbour of the dead guy. She said he was kind of a creep."

"What do you know about him?" I asked, careful not to say his name out loud and breach confidentiality.

"She said he was an ogler and maybe did drugs."

Chandler remarked on a one-centimetre polyp as he traversed the mid-colon and said he would deal with it on the way back. When he reached the end of the colon, the painful part of the procedure was over so I eased off on the sedation. Retracting the scope, he located the polyp again. Sara handed him a wire loop, which he passed around the polyp, shearing it off and cauterizing the base.

Val began to rouse as he was finishing the polypectomy. The sedation was wearing off prematurely. "So, are you a family man, Chandler?" she inquired casually, with four feet of colonoscope inside her bum.

I gave her more sedation. "Sorry, Chandler. On the bright side, she didn't ask you to rate her ass."

"She can shove her ass up her ass," he said.

"She won't remember any of this. Midazolam causes retrograde amnesia. It's strange because all the other benzos cause anterograde amnesia."

Some may say that the colonoscopy suite would be an unappetizing environment to have lunch. I don't eat breakfast before work, but I had packed a muffin, a cheese sandwich and a thermos of coffee. It's entirely possible to brunch sitting off to one side while the surgeon is navigating colons, consuming in stages when there is a spare minute. It wasn't nearly enough calories, but it made me more popular with the surgeons not to take a break.

At the end of the day, I passed the operating room clerk where she was seated at her computer terminal. Penny handed me a small square of paper with a name and phone number written on it. She said that the same woman had called twice trying to get hold of me. She hadn't put the call through because it hadn't seemed urgent. It was a relative of a dead person. Looking at the paper, I saw the name Taylor McGuire and a seven-digit phone number.

I drove to the sub shop in a strip mall close to the hospital that I had been frequenting for over two decades. I hadn't had a real lunch and by now I needed lupper. The proprietor, with whom I was friendly, was serving the counter. She seemed happy most of the time. She was Indian, as was most of her staff. Everyone was wearing Covid masks, so I put one on too.

"Hi Matt."

"Hi Tinky. Still like making subs?"

"Oh yes, I love it," she said.

"Really… What's your favourite sub?"

"I never eat subs. Are you still working or are you retired now?"

"I've got two jobs. I do anesthetics for surgery and I'm a part-time coroner. I got the coroner job for when I retire from the hospital."

She didn't say anything.

"Do you know what that is? I help the police to determine the cause of death if there's a suspicious case or an accident or someone dies alone at home."

"Do you sleep well?"

"Yes. Why?"

"I couldn't do that. All that blood."

"I'm able to keep that in a separate part of my brain. It would be different of course if it was someone related to me."

She looked me over to see if I was telling the truth and then nodded. "What kind of sub would you like?" I got a seafood and a Greek souvlaki in case Katya wondered why I didn't buy her one.

Two derelict freedom-fighters were loitering on the sidewalk partially obstructing the doorway. I adjusted my mask to firmly cover my breathing face holes. As I brushed past them, one of them mock-coughed. This was the ethos now. I would have made a retort, but nothing sprang to mind on the way back to my truck.

Katya wasn't home yet. I dropped the subs on the kitchen table and worked my way through one and a half. Moving to my study, I spread the contents of the file folder for Albert Yantzi on my desk. I picked up the phone to return Taylor's call and got her on the first ring.

"Hi Doctor. Sorry to bother you, but I have some insurance forms for you to fill out," she said enthusiastically.

"Coroners don't ordinarily do that except when there is no one else, like a family doctor, in which case they might. There is a charge if I fill them out for you."

"Oh no problem about the charge. There really is nobody else to do it. My father didn't have a family doctor."

"Did you go over to his apartment?"

"Yes, I was over there yesterday and today cleaning up. I didn't say so earlier, but my father might have done some hard drugs too ten years ago."

"What did he use."

"Oxycodone and meth."

"Did you find anything like that while you were cleaning the apartment?"

"No. I found a life insurance policy naming me as the beneficiary. I was at the insurance broker's office today and they gave me some forms for you to fill out. They want you to write in the cause of death and give me a copy of the death certificate."

"I can't do that because I haven't decided on a cause of death yet. The investigation isn't finished."

"Couldn't you write the preliminary cause of death?"

"The preliminary manner of death is 'undetermined.' Most insurance policies are invalidated if it turns out that the manner of death is suicide." Insurance companies actually need the manner, not cause of death. The five possible manners are natural, accident, suicide, homicide and undetermined. Telling them the cause, like drug overdose or gunshot wound, might breach confidentiality.

"My father would never have killed himself!" Taylor exclaimed. "Mennonites aren't allowed to do that."

"Was he a Mennonite?"

"He left that at age 17. My parents divorced a few years after. Even if you find some drugs in his system, it could have been an accident that he took too much, right?"

"He had been shot in the head, Taylor. And there was a rifle by his side."

"Then it was an accident, or somebody else killed him."

"Where is your mother now, Taylor? Is she still alive?"

"Yes. She's remarried. She lives in Toronto."

Married spouses kill each other, but not long-divorced ones. Estranged spouses also don't qualify as next of kin, so I didn't need to speak with her.

"Did the police interview you?" I asked.

"Yes. Quite a lot."

"Are you a Mennonite too?" She sounded too worldly.

"Yes. McGuire is my married name."

"The police will make a determination as to whether there was any criminality. If they don't suspect foul play, the probable verdict will be suicide. An accident is improbable. Find out if the insurance company would be happy with an undetermined manner of death. They might be if all they need is proof of death."

"Okay."

"I can telephone you when I get the final report from the pathologist who did the autopsy. Their reports are notoriously slow. It might be a few months."

"Okay," she said again. She sounded like an obedient little girl.

Taylor would only get a payout if the manner of death was homicide. It was strange to leave her hoping her father had been murdered in order to get an inheritance. I didn't ask what the payout from the insurance policy would be.

My conversation with Taylor prompted me to email Branko to ask him whether there were any developments in the case. I was interested in whether they had found fingerprints on the rifle. Although Albert Yantzi's prints weren't on file, maybe someone else had left prints. Branko hadn't responded yet to my email from the previous day. It was difficult to know when he was working. I expected he would get back to me whenever he had his next shift.

Chapter 5

Miller, one of the new anesthesiologists at Coventry Hospital, group texted the department to say he had a situation and could someone cover his call tomorrow. He had taken to signing off texts and emails with his name, comma, university degrees, comma, Adjunct Professor of Anesthesia, University of Toronto. The latter was an honorary title, bestowed by the university in return for allowing the occasional medical student or resident to tag along for a few days in the operating room. We all had it or could get it.

I waited for five minutes to see if anyone else volunteered. Unfortunately, I owed him for previously covering for me and felt obligated. No stranger to pretension, I texted him back to say I would do it, signing off as, Matthias Kork, MD, FRCPC, Professor of gastronomy, phrenology, numerology and the rhythm method; lover of puff-pastry, watery melons, prime numbers and positive pregnancy tests. Then I thought, what if he takes it the wrong way, and changed it to Matt.

The first case of the call day was an emergency laparotomy for colonic perforation. There is a one in one thousand risk of perforation during colonoscopy—a little higher if a polypectomy is done during the procedure and the surgeon is at the beginning of his career. The patient was Val from yesterday. She had developed abdominal pain, fever and tenderness overnight and an abdominal X-ray had shown free air outside of the colon.

Val had no recollection of the colonoscopy from the previous day. Retrograde amnesia is one of the benefits of midazolam. You can give it after something happens that you want a patient to forget. She was uncomfortable but not too sick yet. There was a bag of antibiotics attached to her intravenous. As I was putting her to sleep for the surgery, she whispered, "Do a good job," to me, and then announced to the room, "I'll give anyone who buys a house from me a complimentary blowjob."

The surgeon was Chandler again. Since it was daytime, he was expected to deal with his own complications. The general surgeon on call for the day covered after 5 p.m. Chandler made an abdominal incision and quickly found the small hole in the colon. He sewed it closed and then began closing the abdomen. A perforated colon is serious, but there was no obvious poop outside the bowel. The surgery was quick and easy.

Chandler didn't look stressed, but personally I think it would be less stressful for the surgeon if a colleague without the emotional baggage of blame did the repeat procedure when a complication occurred.

"If I had a complication, like a post dural puncture headache from pushing an epidural needle too far, I think I would prefer to have a colleague plug the hole with an epidural blood patch, rather than doing it myself," I said.

Chandler didn't look up from his work or respond.

When he had finished closing, Chandler demurely asked, "Did she give you a blowjob when you bought your house?" He was a proficient surgeon and his mind had moved on.

"I told her I would settle for just the dirty talk," I said. "I think she might also do the blowjob with no preconditions."

Katya had an appointment with Chandler for a colonoscopy in a month. Her father had had colon cancer in his mid-eighties. Because he was older when it was diagnosed, it wasn't supposed to be the hereditary kind of colon cancer. I was wondering whether she would be nervous going to Chandler after I told her about this.

Katya was already asleep when I got home at midnight. Before going to bed, I fiddled with my phone in the kitchen, trying out ring tones to see which was least likely to provoke a sinking feeling in my stomach. After 30 years of taking call, most of them provoked it. I hated the default tone called *Reflection* the most. I still heard it all the time from other peoples' phones. Getting called in the middle of the night meant having to get up and run to intervene in some crisis. I settled on *Crickets,* a retro, low-pitched chirp.

The phone chirped at 3 a.m. when the obstetric ward called. I didn't recognize the caller's voice. It was a new nurse because she sounded like she was reading from a prepared script. She was prepared for any potential challenge I might mount.

They had a patient who was having her fifth baby, previously all vaginal deliveries, eight centimeters dilated, with a history of quick labours and needed an epidural. Epidurals are for treating labour pain. After the first one, labours are progressively shorter with each subsequent child. She was likely to deliver before I ever got there.

"Okay, I'll just come in my pyjamas then. Break all the speed limits. I have to get that needle in her back before the baby comes out."

The nurse didn't respond.

"Okay, I'll come in." I would have to go in any case.

When I arrived at the hospital, the patient had been moved to the operating room as she now needed a Caesarean section because of lack of progression. She actually did need my attention after all. I was glad I had gotten up for a valid reason and was a little ashamed of my sarcasm on the phone. I am only right most of the time.

I met the obstetrician, Adam, in the hallway. Adam was an ex-Bajan, ex-Olympic track athlete. As it turned out, all that physical training had been to acquire stamina for staying up nights to deliver babies. He and I were well acquainted, having been through many endurance trials together.

"Mennonite mother of four, Anna Yantzi, cheerful, non-stop chatty," he said. "She's stuck at nine centimetres. There's no fetal distress, so there's time for you to do a spinal." He wasn't speaking in Bajan patois, so everything was under control.

A spinal anesthetic was the commonest for Caesareans. It was a little safer but more time consuming than a general anesthetic. The baby didn't get an anesthetic with a spinal. Its main potential side effect was lowering maternal blood pressure. The procedure involved injecting local anesthetic between two of the lower lumbar vertebrae, below the level that the spinal cord ended, into the spinal fluid. It would freeze the patient to the mid-chest. Adam's suggesting this meant I could proceed in an organized leisurely fashion.

"The husband doesn't want to come to the O.R., so you'll get some peace, mon," he said.

"More space anyway. I still have to talk to her."

After being wrenched out of my bed, the no-husband-in-the-room information put me in a better mood. Husbands needed reassurance and crowded me at the head of the table. Entering the O.R., I saw a patient with a cherubic face and white bonnet labouring on the operating table. Two Mennonite mid-wives with white bonnets were sitting beside her, talking to distract her. I introduced myself to Anna and made preparations for her anesthetic. The Mennonite ladies were busy sharing information about babies that relatives in Mexico had had.

When I was ready, I shooed the midwives away and Sara, the circulating nurse, got the patient sitting. After passing a spinal needle into her lower back, I saw clear cerebrospinal fluid and injected the freezing. Sara got a pump with phenylephrine, a vasopressor drug, running and I plugged it into her intravenous drip to keep her blood pressure normal.

Once the surgeon started, it was my turn to distract Anna. "So, how did you end up living here? I heard you're from Mexico."

"My husband Caleb lives here."

"He didn't want to come in with you?"

"He is very squeamish."

"How did you meet him?"

"I came up for a three-week holiday."

"Was this like a marriage convention?"

"No. My second cousins live here."

"Was it love at first sight?"

"No."

"Did it develop over time?"

There was a ten-second period of silence. Then she said, "The one I wanted was taken."

I nearly burst out laughing at her refreshing honesty and then suppressed the impulse. This was her personal tragedy. She already had four children with this man. I told her that her secret was safe with me. The baby was delivered and handed off to the obstetric nurses who placed it in an incubator to check it over.

"Beautiful baby. I don't say that to everyone," Sara said as the midwives brought the baby over to show Anna.

"She really doesn't." I nudged Sara with my elbow. "If there is an ugly baby, she'll call it right out."

A porter brought in a ward bed, and everyone in the room helped to slide Anna onto it. Sara and I wheeled Anna down the hall to her room. The husband, who was loitering outside the room, didn't meet my gaze. He was skinny and plain, with a clean-shaven, tanned face and dark hair. He had the typical blue shirt, black pants and wide-brimmed straw hat topping a bowl-shaped hairdo. He looked familiar, but I couldn't place him. Most traditional Mennonites look the same.

Anna Yantzi didn't have provincial health insurance. Coverage is free in Ontario, and secular Mennonites do have health cards. Old Order Mennonites refuse coverage to avoid being beholden to the state. Their men grow beards when they marry, so the Yantzis were something in between traditional and secular. Before leaving, I went to the nursing station to get the husband's full name, plus address and telephone number from the chart. The telephone might be communal rather than personal.

His full name was Caleb Aaron Yantzi. Yantzi or Jantzi, and Yutzi or Jutzi, are very common Mennonite surnames. Mennonites have large families and tend to stay close to each other. If I addressed my bill to both the husband and wife, using their full names, the bill would be more likely to find the right Yantzis. As Mennonites have a patriarchal society, I felt that I was also more likely to get paid if I included the husband in the debt obligation.

I didn't get to bed until 5 a.m., dozing in a semi-startled, ready-to-get-up-and-run state until my call duties ended at 7:30. At that instant, I plunged into a deep sleep, emerging mid-morning with no clear idea of person, place or time. Katya was in the kitchen timing the tea bag in her cup of hot water when I made my entrance.

"Hi," I said. "Sleep well?"

"Yes."

"I didn't"

"Oh no, hon. How come?"

"Hyped-up-on-a-knife's-edge on call."

"You should start making retirement plans. I'm scaling down. I'm two-thirds-time this semester. I'm only teaching two courses."

"I get the day off after a night on call. A man's sense of self-worth is tied to his occupation."

"I don't think most women feel that way. They don't live to work. Their enjoyment of life comes from friends and family."

"Val Papadopolis had surgery yesterday for a perforated colon, which was a complication of colonoscopy. Chandler was the surgeon."

"That's who my family doctor referred me to for my colonoscopy! Do you think I should still go?"

"I think it should be okay. The risk of perforation is one in a thousand. He's had one now, so he should be good for another 999 patients. It might be awkward for me if you cancel. It's up to you. You haven't seen him in his office yet, so maybe he won't know if you cancel with his secretary and go to someone else."

"I don't think I've met him. What's he look like?'

"Tall, thin, soft-spoken, balding."

Katya looked confused. "Who do you recommend?"

"They are all pretty good now. I could get Isaiah. He has the most experience—although we aren't, as you know, on the best of terms."

"Didn't he lose his licence for cocaine possession and a hit-and-run accident?

"He got a plea deal and went to rehab. He's got his licence back now. He's still the best technical surgeon."

"I don't think so."

"I could ask around to see who's good in Somerset."

"Okay."

"Okay, cancel your appointment with Chandler, and I'll do some research. I had an interesting Mennonite patient for a Caesarean overnight."

"Really. What happened?"

"The interesting part was how she found a husband. You know, Mennonites have a problem with a high incidence of congenital birth defects because they inter-marry inside of a small gene pool."

"Right."

"There is also a Mennonite colony in Mexico," I said. "She found a husband at a Mennonite gene-mixer-with-Mexico marriage convention."

"They do that? Where was that?"

"Right here somewhere. Her husband didn't want to attend the delivery, and so we were alone at the head of the table. I asked her conversationally how she met him. She told me about travelling here and when I questioned her more closely, it came out that she was looking over the breeding stock but that she didn't get her first choice. I asked the right questions and she was a truthful person."

"Wow. Wowie, wowie, wow, hon."

"The father of her now five children."

"Cause you know what happens as soon as summer's over? Bingo, bango, bongo, the summer's over," Katya said. "The way you cross-examine people, you should have been a lawyer."

"People usually tell you what's top of mind without much prompting. It just bubbles out. She was actually really nice. The honesty was refreshing."

People like Anna Yantzi have to play with the cards that they are dealt. I printed the bill for Caleb and Anna Yantzi and took it to the mailbox. I wanted to get it out before the obstetrician and hospital sent their bills, in case the Yantzis had limited funds. Mennonites usually say their church will take up a collection for them to make you feel guilty about sending them an invoice. It doesn't work on me.

Chapter 6

Taylor McGuire called me at home in the afternoon. I didn't like that she had my number, but it was unavoidable that as soon as I called her cell phone it would be stored. She said that the life insurance company needed the final, not the preliminary, undetermined, cause of death and a copy of the death certificate. She had a nice voice, pleasant, not wheedling. Could I please hurry up with the paperwork so that she could file her claim.

What ensued was a repeat of our previous telephone conversation. I told her that the timing was largely out of my control. She could apply in writing for a copy of the coroner's report now. I would upload the report as soon as the final pathology and toxicology reports were available and the police investigation was done, which might take up to a few months. She absorbed this quietly. There was disappointment in her voice when she reluctantly said goodbye.

I was back in the operating room the next morning doing an orthopaedic list with Joshua White. He is an orthopedic surgeon whose wardrobe is mostly sweat pants and beer T-shirts. He doesn't have to dress to impress. We were doing four total joint replacements—two hips and two knees—all elderly patients getting shiny, new, titanium-alloy metal parts.

The circulating nurse Kristiaan and I were in the O.R. getting ready. Josh entered the room and said, "Namaste bitches."

"Namaste," we echoed back.

"Ready for some fun and frolic?" he asked.

"Yes," we echoed wearily.

Josh walked over to the computer terminal to tune in a music stream, which he cranked to volume level eleven.

"What beach would you like to be at today?" Josh asked us. "If you think nice thoughts, you will have nice dreams." He was teasing Kristiaan who said this to nearly every patient as they were going to sleep for an operation.

"I'm not saying that today," Kristiaan corrected. "Matt's giving everyone a spinal."

That was the plan, although it was sometimes easier said than done. The spinal anesthetic for these surgeries involved inserting a needle between the bones of the lower back to freeze the patient from the waist down. Elderly patients had less pain and confusion postoperatively with spinal anesthetics. They were sometimes difficult to do in old people if the spaces between their lumbar vertebrae had collapsed or were filled with boney spurs.

"Do you mind turning the music down a bit, Josh?" I wanted the elderly patients to be able to hear me. They would be sitting, facing away from me, for their spinal anesthetic procedures.

Although they were both challenging, the spinals were successful for the initial two cases. The first patient was so old and arthritic that I had to walk the needle off the bones at several levels to find an opening. The second patient was so obese that I couldn't feel the spinous processes through the skin and had to use an ultrasound machine to locate them. Our cylindrical tourniquet didn't fit the conical shape of his thigh. This actually resulted in more bleeding as arterial blood still entered the leg and only venous return was blocked.

Josh operated through cascading blood for a while but eventually asked for the tourniquet to be let down and worked without it. This actually improved the operating conditions, and he launched into a loud un-self-conscious falsetto sing-along with Roxanne on Spotify. When it ended, he said, "So, there were three old ladies on a bench outside a nursing home. A male streaker runs by. The first one faints, the second one seizes, the third one couldn't reach."

It was an old joke. There was no response from the room.

"Huh? Huh?" Josh said encouragingly.

"No," Kristiaan said.

"Okay then," Josh said. "How do you fit four hookers on a chair?"

Nobody knew. People stopped what they were doing to hear the answer. I looked nervously at the patient, who had been sedated, but not guaranteed unconscious, to see if any of this was affecting him.

"Turn the chair upside down," Josh said, and this did get a laugh.

Happily, the patient didn't give any sign of having heard. The two metal joint components got hammered and cemented in place and Josh began to close the wound. This staunched the flow of blood. "He'll get better TV reception now." Josh said as he stapled the skin closed.

Sara came into the O.R. with a written message for me from the desk clerk.

Josh looked up from his work. "Gentlemen, put your hands together. All the way from Three Rivers, Quebec. She's got a sparkle in her eye. It's the lovely, Cinnamon!"

"What's all that red stuff on the floor, Josh?" Sara said.

"I'm painting the Mona Lisa."

"More like a Jackson Pollock," Kristiaan said.

"Or a Charlie Manson," Sara said.

She handed me a message on a square of paper, which I unfolded and read. There was a woman named Taylor McGuire in the waiting room to see me.

"The O.R. clerk says that she's hot," Sara said.

"Define hot."

"Blonde hair, blue eyes, big tits," Sara said. There was a note of jealousy.

"She's the daughter of one of my coroner cases. I've talked to her on the phone several times already. She's beginning to be a pain."

"I think you're apt to change your mind when you see her."

"Did you see her?"

"I had a peek."

"Okay, well, if you recommend her... I'm about half an hour from finishing here. Could you tell her that?"

"Yes."

I finished my case and delivered the patient with Kristiaan to the recovery room. We got the patient settled and he said, "Good jokes in there."

"Did any of that bother you?" I asked.

"It helped to pass the time. He's not much of a singer."

"If the surgeon is singing during your procedure, you can relax because everything is going well."

Making my way out to the waiting room, I picked her out right away—thirtyish, blonde hair, blue eyes, heavy makeup, well endowed. When I announced her name, she met my gaze and stood up. She was about five feet, eight inches tall, wearing a form-fitting, knee-length pencil skirt and a white satin blouse with the top two buttons undone.

"Hello Dr. Kork. I hope you don't mind me bothering you at work. I didn't know how else to see you."

"That's okay. I'm just between cases. Come in for a moment."

I ushered her into a side office and asked her to take a seat. "How did you know where to find me?" I asked.

"The police told me. Your office address isn't listed, so I called them to find out." She opened her purse and brought out a sheaf of pages. "These are the insurance forms we were talking about."

"I don't have an office address. My primary occupation is working in an operating room as an anesthesiologist. I could do the insurance forms for you, but there is not much point if the verdict is suicide. I'm pretty sure the policy would be voided."

"How much is the charge for completing them?" She opened her wallet and took out a wad of bills.

"Put your wallet away. The charge will be about $75, depending on the time it takes to do them. Why don't I just hold onto them for now. I'll do them when the police have finished their investigation and then I'll send you a bill."

She looked disappointed. She was certainly a pleasure to behold.

"I'm sorry. I have to go back to work now," I said, gathering up the papers. "The surgeries here are very tightly booked. Can you leave your full mailing address with the clerk at the front? Can you find your way back out?"

"Yes, I think so." Her lips were painted bright red. When she stood up, she looked like a fashion model.

I pointed in the direction that we had come and took a last look at her before turning and rushing back to interview the next patient waiting for surgery.

After work, I found Katya at home seated at the kitchen counter with a teacup, doing the newspaper crossword.

"Eff why eye, I won't be having dinner with you tonight." She took a sip of her brew.

"Do you have eater's remorse?"

"No. I'm going to movie club. Everyone brings a little plate of something to do with the movie theme. It adds up."

"Am I invited?"

"No. It's just women."

"Why just women?"

"Because that's sort of the point."

Katya belonged to a movie club, two book clubs, a neighbour-ladies' walking club, a visiting her sister club and played golf once a week with golf clubs. The common theme was that the clubs excluded men.

"I guess I could get a sub."

"That's a good idea."

"Why aren't husbands invited? Men like movies too," I said.

"Why don't you start your own club? Martha's husband belongs to a poker club. Why don't you join that?"

"I don't like games of chance or gambling. We used to have social events as couples. Did you foresee, when you got married, that in 30 years you would be pursuing a social life entirely excluding your husband?

"Well, women have had to do it without their husbands for so long that they've just gotten used to it. Martha, the organizer, said not to invite husbands because they talk over you."

"Do you agree with that?"

"You went to the hockey banquet without me."

"I invited you."

"You said that only newly-weds bring their wives to those. I want you to develop some interests outside work. Take up golf. I don't want you following me around after you retire."

"Would we play golf together?" I wondered wistfully.

"Theoretically, why not?"

Katya doesn't want me following her around like some younger brother. Women are far better than men in planning a social life in and after middle age. The future didn't look good for me. Eye will be sofa king lonely. I have work and sports, but when I'm too old to play sports, I'll be watching instructional poker videos on YouTube.

Branko called me in person that evening. He knew all about the autopsy result because he had attended it. He said that when they opened the lever action of the Winchester, they found one spent cartridge in the chamber. There were no other cartridges in the magazine. They couldn't say that the bullet was definitely fired from the Winchester because it was so fragmented.

"It was probably fired from the Winchester," Branko said. "If it was fired from a high-velocity weapon, you wouldn't have found the bullet in his head, and half his head would be missing."

"The pathologist said the shot was from six inches to a foot away," I said. "That doesn't support suicide. I think if he wanted to kill himself, he would have pressed the gun up against his head so there would be no possibility of survival with a debilitating injury."

"Yeah. Gunpowder stippling means it wasn't a contact wound. There was a partial palm print on the rifle, but they couldn't match it to Albert. His hands were too swollen and decomposed to get finger or palm prints. There were no prints on file for him either."

"Where on the rifle was the print?" I asked.

"It's actually uncommon to find useable prints on guns. The palm print was on the stock and oriented upwards. That suggests someone pointing the barrel at themselves and pulling the trigger with their thumb. Of course, we don't know when the print was left there."

"The rifle was lying exactly parallel to the body. That doesn't fit with suicide either, does it?"

"It's suspicious."

"I'm leaning more toward homicide than suicide," I said. "Also, I don't like that he shot himself right in the earhole. Most people wouldn't want to hear the shot coming." I was coming around to Taylor's way of thinking.

"Cause and manner of death is your call, as coroner. We'll keep investigating. We don't have motive or a suspect if it's murder."

"I'll call it undetermined in my preliminary report. You've seen a lot more of these than I have. What does your gut tell you?"

"Not in Canada. I saw some things in Serbia," Branko said grimly. "I've still got an open mind."

The receptionist at Dr. Doyle's dental office called me a few minutes later. She said that she had found some dental X-rays from 20 years ago in their office basement. That was what she meant by off-site storage. From the hour, she must have been working overtime.

After thanking her profusely, I gave her the postal address of the Centre of Forensic Sciences in Toronto and asked her to have the X-rays and any other records couriered there. I told her that I would fax her an Authority to Seize to cover her legally. She agreed without asking who would pay the courier fees, or for that matter, for her time. This was nice because I didn't have a ready answer.

Chapter 7

A friend is someone who would help you move. A best friend is someone who would help you move a dead body. That would describe Sean Feeney. Before he retired, he used to teach at Katya's school and I knew him through Katya. He came from a family that was associated with the IRA and the troubles in Ireland. His current occupation was running a bed and breakfast hotel in Coventry.

He had seen an ad in the Globe and Mail newspaper for a Paul Simon concert. He called me up to ask if I wanted to go with him.

"It should be grand, savage in fact." Sean was born in Ireland.

"I didn't know you were a fan," I said. "Is it just the bros or are wives included in the invitation?"

"Sinead told me that she and Katya are going to movie club together that night."

"Do you think we should form our own movie club?"

"Do you mean a porno movie club?"

"No."

'Then, no."

I had seen the ad in the Globe too and had been considering going. The trouble with the idea was fighting traffic and finding a parking spot in downtown Toronto. Sean said it might be Paul's farewell tour, and that clinched it. A week later, we were boarding the VIA Rail train together on our way to the concert. We had to abide by the train schedule, which put us in downtown Toronto with 45 minutes to spare. It wasn't enough time to do a restaurant meal so we got stale sandwiches on board.

We walked to the theatre and arrived early enough to suffer through the warm-up act. Having splurged for the best seats available, we were seated fifth row from the front of the theatre. We were both over six feet in height, but Sean was heavier. I let him have the aisle seat, so he could man-sprawl his legs.

When Paul came on stage, he immediately launched into his first number. He was greeted with a standing ovation, the first of many.

"He still looks pretty good. How old is he now?" I asked Sean.

"Close to 80 probably."

"He better not drop on stage. I like him, but I'm not giving him mouth to mouth."

"He probably has a medical team he travels with. You can be his coroner if things don't turn out."

Mid-way through the show, a middle-aged woman, with husband in tow, danced from the cheap seats at the back of the auditorium down the aisle and over Sean's legs to the front. Her husband seemed uncomfortable but was dragged along to the foot of the stage. As she waved her hands above her head, she was impeded by a large swinging purse slung over her shoulder with the shoulder strap diagonally between her breasts. Bringing the purse was the rational part of her spontaneous exuberance. They were soon joined by conga lines of dancers moving toward the front to improve their view.

A few security people took up stride-jump positions halfway along the theatre's centre aisle. They attempted to obstruct the momentum of the conga dancers and return them to their seats, but they didn't have the numbers to control the outer aisles. Most of the audience was standing now to be able to see. A group of three buxom young women had set up camp below the stage to our right. They held their hands aloft and danced competitively for Paul's attention. Paul was now pudgy, bald and old, and it was a fine tribute.

When the encores were over, Sean stood up and said, "No banter. All business. Paul didn't really tell me anything about himself."

"He's shy."

"Okay, let's go home, boyo. We have to catch the last train so I can get up early enough to make six rounds of eggs Benedict."

"But you're the B 'n B *proprietor*! How many guests do you have?"

"Four at the moment. The guests like my cooking. I'm also back supply teaching as a high school guidance counsellor. I do a day or two here and there to pay for rock concerts."

Outside the theatre, we stopped to buy fancy hot dogs from a street vendor. A group of pretty girls stood behind us in line and asked for bottled water. They looked familiar. I asked whether they were at the Paul Simon concert and hadn't I seen them dancing at the front? They enthusiastically said yes, you have to. I asked whether they thought Paul Simon had noticed them. Nervous giggles only.

It was then I recognized Taylor McGuire. She was wearing a black leather mini-skirt, a white halter top with a blue-jean jacket and a blingy, silver chain necklace.

"Hi Taylor," I said. It's me, Dr. Kork."

"Hi! Yes, I know."

"Are you here with friends or family?" None of them looked like Mennonites.

"These are my friends—Piper and Parker. I don't have any real blood family left, except for a half-brother."

"Hello Piper. Hi Parker. I didn't know you had a brother, Taylor."

"Caleb's a few years younger than me. I'm pretty sure he would never come to a concert like this."

"Would his full name be Caleb Yantzi then?

"Yes. I was a Yantzi. McGuire is my married name, but I'm separated."

"Did your brother just have a baby?"

She hesitated. "I'm not sure. We're not close. I think he did. That would make five. He first told me not to tell we were related, but now he doesn't mind."

"Not to tell who?" I asked.

"Oh, nobody in particular."

I surveyed the group. They were dressed much like Taylor. Piper and Parker looked eager to move on.

Not wanting to discuss insurance claims again, I said, "I'll mail you those papers we talked about when they're ready, Taylor. Have a great night, ladies."

There was a hurried chorus of byes. They linked arms and their chatter receded down the sidewalk toward Yonge Street.

Sean asked what that was about.

"She's the estranged daughter of a decomposing corpse in a coroner's investigation."

"One of them seemed to be making googly eyes at you, boyo."

"She wants me to fill out life insurance papers."

"Is she pressuring you to commit insurance fraud, Matthew?"

"More like enticing. Do you think Paul Simon noticed them?"

"I think that he did."

By the time I got home, Katya was already in bed. I opened the bedroom windows and turned on the fan for white noise. I arranged my six pillows for ergonomic sleeping excellence—three under my head, two between my legs and one to support my upper arm lying on my side, like a patient positioned for surgery. All this activity may have wakened her.

"How was the Paul Simon concert?" she asked.

I softened my voice to a whisper. "Excellent. He had assembled a big jazz band of mostly black guys to back him, did a lot of tunes from *Graceland* and signed boobs for 15 minutes at the end. Go back to sleep."

I crawled in beside Katya, using her as a seventh pillow to put a little flex in my lower arm.

In the morning, Katya observed that we were running low on essentials. It was my turn to do the grocery shopping. I got my four green plastic bins and loaded them into the back of my truck. There were four supermarkets in Coventry, catering to all the different price points. I usually went to the most expensive one because food is the cheapest thing you can put in your body.

Tooling down the produce aisle, I noticed Val Papadopolis from the corner of my eye. I tried shifting my cart to an angle where she wouldn't notice me, but it was too late. She pulled her cart up beside mine, and I suddenly remembered that she must have recently got out of hospital.

"Hi Val. I'm relieved to see you're looking well."

"Oh, I'm right as rain. You know, your wife dropped in on an open house I was hosting last week. She said she was just browsing and more interested in moving to Toronto some day. There is a condo right downtown with a view of the lake in the distance that you should have a look at. I thought of you immediately when I heard about it. A colleague of mine in Toronto has the listing—close to everything, walking distance to the theatres on King Street West."

"I'm definitely not interested."

"They are entertaining blind bids starting next Monday. The floor is one point five million. It would be a great investment until you're ready to move."

"Nice. What would your referral fee be?"

"Ten percent of five percent."

"Still no."

"You'll be bidding against Taylor McGuire. You know her, I think."

"How do you know that?"

She laughed. "Oh, you know, small town."

Taylor was already spending the insurance money. Given his lifestyle, I wouldn't have thought Albert Yantzi would have qualified for a very large death benefit.

When I got home, I asked Katya whether she had been talking to Val Papadopolis about condos in Toronto.

"Not really. How did that coroner call with the decomposed body turn out?" she asked.

"Well, he had bullet fragments in his head."

"Really! So, did he commit suicide or did someone shoot him?"

"As you might know, the five manners of death are natural, accident, suicide, homicide or undetermined. It's one of the last four."

"That's fascinating. Tell me more about the five manners."

I noticed we had moved away from talking about real estate. Katya harboured a not-so-secret dream of moving to Toronto some day, an idea to which I was vehemently opposed. I had grown up in a suburb of Toronto. Big cities are the loneliest places to live. Nothing worth attending is actually easy to get to, unless you live in a condo downtown of course.

My sister still lived in Toronto, so Katya and I went once a year at Christmas. I didn't really keep up with anyone from my old neighbourhood, except for Dolly. My last real connection was severed when a close friend from high school died of cancer. I went to his celebration of life, held in a bar in Scarborough, with pizza and wings and mingled with mostly strangers.

Dolly was an older woman who lived across the street from the house I grew up in. She claimed an emotional connection, but it was tenuous. I had stayed in her house once overnight. A motorcycle ran into me when I was cruising through my old neighbourhood to see how it had changed. Dolly took me in and put a Band-Aid on my forehead. I didn't feel like I should be driving anymore that night.

She got my telephone number when the police left the business card I had given them at her house. They copied the information into a notebook from the card and must have forgotten it. She was childless and seemed to latch onto me. The card listed my cell number and fax number, which was the same as my landline. She dialed the fax number and got me.

She called me about once a year, and if she called, there was no getting off the phone for an hour. We had nothing really to say to one another and I think she was just lonely. If I saw her number on the call display, I was tempted to let it go to voice mail, but I usually picked up. I hadn't heard from her in a while.

After the groceries were put away, I texted Branko. "Did you know that Taylor McGuire has a half-brother, Caleb Yantzi? Do you have his contact information?"

He responded, "No. We didn't know there were any other siblings."

I typed, "I'm going to call him for more background information. Maybe you should interview him. I have a telephone number, but it might be communal. Also, he owes me money."

He responded, "Give me the number, but it likely warrants an in-person visit."

Chapter 8

Mennonites normally pay their bills promptly, so I was surprised when Caleb and Anna didn't. One month had elapsed since I had sent them the first bill. I printed off a second notice and added a hand-written line at the bottom. I wrote that I wouldn't expect them to work for free, receiving services without paying for them was theft and wasn't that a sin. I thought that might touch a nerve. It was their own choice not to have free-for-the-asking provincial health insurance.

Needing a break, I wondered off to the kitchen to make some breakfast. Madame Fifi was standing beside her basket, pre-occupied with growling at and biting at the blanket at the bottom.

"She's really not the same species as us, is she," I said to Katya.

"She has different priorities."

The phone rang and I glanced at the call display. There was a long string of numbers filling two lines on the screen. I picked up on speakerphone and said nothing. After about 15 seconds, I heard a connection being made.

A heavily accented South-Asian male voice said, "Hello sir. This is Canada RCMP calling. Ve have detected some suspicious activity on your VISA card. Did you make a purchase for $1049.49 yesterday in Singapore?"

"My wife shops all over the internet. Katya, did you make a purchase for $1049.49 in Singapore yesterday?"

Putting on her most demented voice, Katya said, "I bought some nose-hair clippers for you yesterday, hon. Could that be it?"

"She said, yes," I said into the phone.

"No sir. Nose-hair clippers do not cost $1049.99. You are a victim of credit card fraud."

Katya moved closer to the phone. "Could I speak to Raj please?"

"There is no Raj here," the voice said.

"I spoke with Raj the last time," Katya insisted.

"Raj has the day off today."

"Well, what's your name then?" Katya asked.

Katya reached into the drawer under the phone and pulled out the Indian food take-out menu we kept there.

"My name is Sergeant Terry McKinnon," he said confidently.

"Okay then, Sergeant," Katya croaked. "I'll have two samosas, onion bhajee, the lamb korma, prawn biriyani, chicken vindaloo, sag paneer…"

Slowly and methodically, she proceeded to read the entire first page of the menu, not allowing Sergeant McKinnon to interrupt her.

When she had finished, there was a pause. Then, I heard, "That is a lot of food, Madame."

"I like leftovers for the grandchildren," Katya said.

"How would you like to pay? May I have your VISA card number please?"

"Just one moment." Katya jostled some cutlery in the kitchen sink and then dropped a large pot on top. "Are you ready?—4—1,2,3—4—5—6—7,8…"

He hung up before Katya could finish displaying her command of sequential numbers.

"How did you know he was Indian?" I asked. "He could have been Pakistani, Sri Lankan or Bangladeshi."

"I didn't, but everyone loves Indian food."

"They always call on landlines on weekdays because only old people are home and have landlines," I said.

"Shame on them for taking advantage of old people," Katya said.

"You should have ordered in Polish."

Madame Fifi was now standing beside her basket barking at it. Katya went over, removed and refolded her blanket and lay it flat in the basket. Madame Fifi stopped barking and settled on it.

"She was upset because the blanket wasn't smooth. She's not so different from you. You don't know how to make beds either," Katya said.

"Bichon Frisé dogs are neat freaks. We're both feigning incompetence."

A week later, I received a letter with the address on a small, square envelope hand-scrawled in blue ink. The same scrawl was on a sheet of note paper folded in four inside:

Taylor told Anna who told me you say my father shot himself. You are so very wrong. He did not kill himself. If you check his blood you will probably see that he had lots of drugs in him. He was murdered by drug dealers because he was a drug dealer too.

It was signed Caleb Yantzi. That was more than a little interesting. I forwarded the contents of the letter to Branko by email and then wrote, "Is there any evidence to support this?"

Branko called me at home that evening. "Hey Matt. I got your email today. We paid Caleb a visit last week, and he told us the same thing, about his father being murdered."

"He might be pushing for a murder verdict to collect on life insurance. Suicide wouldn't do him any good."

"Is he a beneficiary?"

"I don't know. I thought you might," I said.

"I'll find out. Do you think he would kill his own father for insurance money and then be stupid enough to report on himself?"

"I don't know him that well. I know he wasn't his wife Anna's first choice of husband."

"Did you get the toxicology report back for Albert?" Branko wanted to know.

"Not yet. I don't know why it takes so long. A private lab produces results within a few days."

"Well, let me know as soon as you do get it."

"Did you get any proof that Caleb is really Albert's son?" I asked.

"He's Albert's son all right. They showed us family photos and his wife backed him up."

"That makes him Taylor's half-brother. Was she in the pictures?"

"They said she was there," Branko said, "but she was a little kid, so I don't know that it was actually her."

"Did he offer any proof that his father was murdered?"

"Feelings. Nothing more than feelings. His father was a drug dealer. Mennonites don't commit suicide. Drug dealers get murdered... Albert didn't have a criminal record. That's unlikely for a drug dealer."

"I know for a fact that Mennonites do commit suicide." I had had a case recently.

"Doesn't everyone."

"I think that although Taylor was estranged from Albert, she and Caleb are still in touch with one another," I said. "Taylor said that Caleb initially told her not to mention him and then changed his mind. They may be cooking something up together to get the insurance money sooner."

"Could be. When are you going to bring in your coroner's verdict?"

"When I get the tox and the final report from the pathologist."

"Well, this entire thing is in limbo then. I'll keep on at my end. I'll check into how long the life insurance policy has been in effect. Let me know when you get the tox back." Branko rang off.

This whole conversation was unsatisfactory. I was goal oriented and I wanted results, especially if this was a murder investigation. In all my years in Coventry, I had never had a murder case. If we were investigating a murder, we should be doing it more quickly and proficiently. I emailed Taylor to ask whether, after going through her father's apartment, she had found anything to indicate that he was suicidal or any evidence that threats had been made against his life.

Taylor emailed me the next day that she had found a notebook that her father Albert had used for recording his thoughts. She had taken a picture of the last two pages and attached it to her message. It showed two lined sheets of paper bound with a spiral metal coil. Handwritten in blue pen was:

Change the law to something.
Heaven help the helpful.
Don't look at me unless you're perfect.
Have a heart, hug a horse.
Winter is coming. Are you?
If you come over for dinner, I'll make plates.

Albert had pretensions to profundity. On the facing page, he had written:

If you are reading this book, you will know that I am dead. My life insurance policy is in the drawer in the kitchen. It is all in order and paid up. I want my loving daughter Taylor to be in charge of getting rid of my stuff. Taylor, I am sorry for the bad times and I love you more than my life. Please do not cry for me because I am in a better place with no worries or fears where I will be a better person.

Taylor, please talk to Caleb and Anna who you will remember as your brother and his wife. They will show you how to live like a good Mennonite. It is the best way to be happy and stay out of trouble if you want to go home. I wish I had never left. The apartment is full of all junk but the life insurance is good.

The entries could possibly be construed as suicidal. Taylor hadn't made any comment on them. Her having sent me this was an indication of her honesty because it was prejudicial to her insurance claim. I emailed her back to ask if Caleb was also a beneficiary on their father's policy.

Another week passed, and then I got an email that a confidential document had been sent to me by encrypted email on the coroners' website. Unlocking the document revealed it to be the toxicology report for Albert Yantzi. In their usual snail's-pace fashion, it had taken six weeks to arrive.

The report showed that there was a qualitative presence of hydromorphone, which is a narcotic, and flubromazolam, a benzodiazepine tranquilizer like Valium or Xanax. This was interesting because flubromazolam was a designer drug, not prescribed anywhere. Qualitative meant they couldn't asses the amount of drug, only that it was present. In the presence of severe decomposition, toxicology can only ever be qualitative. The assessment was done on a piece of liver as there was no blood or vitreous eye fluid left.

Both of the drugs that were identified could be taken by mouth. The lack of syringes or other drug paraphernalia like pipes or spoons in Albert Yantzi's apartment pointed to his having done that. Since he died of a gunshot wound, I didn't know what relevance the hydromorphone and flubromazolam had to his death. Perhaps they impaired his judgement, or maybe he didn't want to feel the bullet when he pulled the trigger.

The presence on toxicology of a non-prescription drug might be corroboration that Taylor and Caleb's father really was a drug dealer or involved with drug dealers. He didn't look prosperous enough to be a dealer, or pay life insurance premiums. As he had no criminal record, it was more likely that he was simply a user.

I forwarded the toxicology information to Branko with the secure email on the coroners' website. This was the proper way to do it. Regular email wasn't considered secure. Fax, landline calls and encrypted email were considered secure. Not knowing whether he would get an automated alert, I also sent a manual alert to his police email address.

When I entered the toxicology information into Albert Yantzi's preliminary coroner's report, the website prompted me to complete missing data fields, including how the decedent was identified. We still didn't have a positive identification for Albert. I called Ron Rasmussen's work number and left a message for him to call me.

Ron got back to me later that day. The pathologist said that their forensic dentist had been unable to make an identification based on the dental records couriered from Dr. Doyle's office. There weren't enough remaining teeth. Post-mortem X-rays of the chest or sinuses can be distinctive but hadn't proved useful either because Albert didn't have any old X-rays to compare them with. Ron seemed rushed. With his busy workload, the case had dimmed in importance.

I called Richard Tull, my Regional Supervising Coroner, to ask whether we should proceed with DNA analysis on Albert Yantzi's hair and toothbrush. He said that that was very expensive. We could go with presumptive identification. The decedent was in a locked apartment and who else would it be.

Chapter 9

It was Wednesday afternoon and therefore time for doctors' hockey. We were playing into June now. I inventoried my hockey equipment as I packed the stuff into the bag from the wooden stand it was drying on in the basement. It took two days to dry and a week for the smell to dissipate. I always took note of the weight of the bag as I hefted it over my shoulder. It was a pain to arrive with only one skate or elbow pad.

Needing every playing advantage, I removed the old gashed tape from the blades of my two hockey sticks. I carefully retaped them so they were clean and smooth and threw the hockey bag and sticks into the back of my SUV. After finding a parking spot outside Coventry Arena, I fished my wallet out of my pocket and hid it under the seat of the car. The rink assumed no responsibility.

The electronic notice board in the entranceway showed the change-room assignments. It read, "DOCTORS HOCKEY, 3 PM, ROOM 6." The cacophony of voices rose in volume as I approached our room. I pushed open the door and tossed my hockey sticks into a corner by the door with all the others. There were eight or nine doctors and a couple of drug reps already in the room in various stages of undress.

I took a seat beside Joshua Smith, who was the one of the best players in our group.

"Namaste," he said.

"Hi. What colour sweater are you wearing today?"

"I was thinking red. You?"

"I'm leaning toward red."

I looked around to see what colour sweater the other skilled players were putting on. There were only four or so that mattered. They had to be divided roughly equally between the two teams. Ordinary players could put on either red or white, depending on their preference, as long as the numbers balanced out. It was a toss-up which colour to choose today. Players of various abilities were still arriving. Josh, the very best player, was wearing red, and it was more fun to play for the winning side, but he seldom passed the puck.

Zack, who was the organizer, stood up to speak. "Okay, listen up everyone. The rink manager approached me last week and told me that no alcohol is to be consumed under any circumstances in the change rooms—that it contravenes the liquor licence laws and they could be fined if anyone does. He was really serious. No more beers after the game."

"I play with cops on Tuesdays and I can tell you they still bring cases of beer into the change room," a family doctor named Paul said.

"So, no more beers under any circumstances," Zack said. He then pulled a case of beer from his hockey bag, put it under the bench and covered it with a towel. The sound of laughter rippled through the room.

People began to file out the door. I had forgotten my phone on my belt and hid it in the bottom of my hockey bag inside a sock. I filled up my water bottle and shoved it into one hockey glove and my car keys into the other. Panic buttons on key fobs can allow thieves to find your vehicle in the parking lot. Grabbing my two sticks from the corner and cradling the gloves, I staggered down the corridor and onto the ice.

We had more than a full complement of players. With six players on each bench, there was more than one substitute for each skater on the ice. I was initially worried I might not get enough ice time, but that changed abruptly. For a reason I couldn't discern, Josh exchanged jerseys with a player on the white team. Having put on a red shirt, we were now on opposing teams. As a red defenceman, I was gasping for air, trying to stem the flood of white team goals.

Arriving back in the room, it was easy to see who had played for the winning side. Although everyone was talkative and flushed, the victors were more boisterous. Jeremiah Chang, our red-team, Chinese, Buddhist, pediatrician goalie was peeling off his pads, which diminished his bulk by 50 per cent, back to a slim Asian man. I would ordinarily have congratulated him for a good game. Having let in so many goals, it didn't seem appropriate.

Jeremiah was in any case pre-occupied—fumbling with his pants pockets, then the pockets of his coat. Then he emptied the contents of his hockey bag onto the floor. "Someone has stolen my cell phone," he announced.

The room got quiet as everyone looked for their phone. Four more players announced that their phones were missing. They were the players who had been sitting closest to the door. Mine was gone too.

"Did anyone lock the door? Who was the last one out?" Josh asked.

"I left last. There was no room key in here," Jeremiah said.

"Isn't that the third time you've had your phone stolen, Jeremiah?" someone asked. "You should just leave your phone out on top of your hockey bag with a note to the thief to use it responsibly."

"I saw a yellow-haired teenage kid with a ballcap and hoodie and no hockey equipment hanging around the corridor," Paul said.

Jeremiah said he was going home to use the *find-my-phone* feature from his home computer. Many of the players who still had their phones or didn't bring them opened beers. The ones who lost their phones weren't in the mood and left. I waited around to see what would happen with Jeremiah.

Twenty minutes later, Jeremiah called Zack to say there was no signal from his phone. Someone thought that some brands kept broadcasting their location even after they were turned off. Zack got a call from Paul a few minutes later to say he had located his phone at an address in Coventry and was parked in front of the building. The thief must not have known how to turn off a Samsung. Zack advised him to call police and not to attempt to enter the premises.

The address was Gleeson Court, a subsidized housing complex that I had visited several times in my role as coroner. Longevity is related to postal code. Cruising over there, I saw Paul in his parked car, outside of one of a row of low-rise apartment buildings. I got out and asked him if he could tell which unit our phones were in, but of course he had no idea. We stood there waiting until a police vehicle pulled up beside us twenty minutes later.

The two cops listened while we reported on our grief. One of them went in through the front door and the other to the back of the building. As Paul and I approached, we witnessed the cop at the back apprehend a suspect as he was rushing out with a pillow case. I could see he was a skinny teenager with sand-coloured greasy hair, wearing a baseball cap.

"Okay, you stupid goof. Give back the phones," the cop said.

"Do you have a search warrant?"

The cop grabbed the pillow case from him. "I have probable cause, asshole." He opened the pillow case exposing a cache of phones. "You two recognize your phones?"

The stupid goof decided it was time to go for a run. I was pissed enough to grab him roughly by the hood of his hoodie, slowing him up while the cop handcuffed him.

"Thanks doc," the cop said.

"The cuffs are too tight."

"You'll get used to them, asshole." The second cop had joined us.

Paul and I began rooting around in the pillow case looking for our phones.

"I'm sorry doctors, but we have to keep them temporarily as evidence."

The second cop took me aside. "Follow me to the station, Dr. Kork. We'll photograph your phone and get you to sign for it. The other guy might have to wait a day or two." He had apparently recognized me.

"What's your name, goofball?" the second cop demanded.

The goofball's name was Tyson Gruber. Tyson is a name for children of fans of ear-biting troglodytes. Although he was only 15, he was known to police. They told me he had no visible means of support and that they would get child services involved.

When I got home, dinner was on the table. Katya had already eaten.

"Thanks for cooking," I said.

"It's cold. You were gone a long time."

"I've been everywhere, man. I would have called you, but my phone was stolen at the arena."

"Oh no! And you just got the newest $1500 Apple iPhone."

"I got it back. I tracked down the teenage thief and made a citizen's arrest, using only necessary force."

"Did you really? My hero."

"There's a find-your-phone app on the newest phones."

"You might have been able to avoid being on call if you hadn't found it right away," Katya said.

"Not everyone got their phone back. Most of them were held as evidence. The cop recognized me."

"That must have engendered some bad feelings amongst the people who didn't get their phone."

65

"No. They know I'm a VIP," I replied. "Also, the police returned it surreptitiously so the other victims didn't see."

"Who was the thief? I might know him."

"His last name was Gruber."

"I had a Tyson Gruber in my class last year," Katya said.

"That's the guy. Skinny, greasy long blonde hair, hoodie, baseball cap?"

"That's him," Katya said.

"I would have punched him out, but there were too many witnesses. Mike Tyson said that everyone has a plan until they get a punch in the mouth, which is what Tyson Gruber deserves. Was he a problem student?"

"No. He was an average student, but he was actually nice."

"Did things mysteriously go missing from the classroom?"

"Nothing that I noticed. He comes from a dysfunctional family. I think it's just him and his father, who looks very sketchy. He showed up on parent-teacher night blaming all the teachers for his son's grades.

"You should have smacked him upside the head."

"You're in a violent mood."

Since I hadn't contributed to the dinner preparation, it was my job to wash and put away the pots and pans and fill the dishwasher. Katya was sitting on the couch with her feet up, reading, with Madame Fifi, who officially wasn't allowed on furniture, curled up beside her.

I settled into an arm chair across the room. "What's that you're reading?"

"Just a book for book club."

"Who chose this month's book?"

"Pamela."

"Who's that?"

"She lives down the street."

That didn't mean too much to me. Katya knew everyone on our street and what their house looked like.

"We should have a party for when you retire at the end of the year," I said. Who would you like me to invite? Can you make list?"

"I decided it might be too jarring to retire completely. I'm going to go half-time next term. We can celebrate that. My sister of course. The teachers at school. We don't see your sister very much."

"We're a little far from Toronto to expect my sister to visit. She seems to be busy with her grandchildren Charlotte and Oliver."

"Yes, those are the noms du jour."

"What is it with names that are also professions?" I asked. "Taylor, Piper, Parker... Hunter, Chandler."

"Carter, Mason, Miller, Fletcher, Tyler," Katya said. "I see that at school. The name fashions cycle about every decade. It was professions in the aughts."

"Okay, let's have a party. Don't forget to invite Painter, Plumber and Electrician. May I see what is so engrossing about what you are reading?"

Katya handed me the book and I scanned the page:

How could she have known when she had seen Robert trotting past on horseback in his jaunty brocade uniform jacket that he would be the one? His jaw was square and his jet-black hair fell in a wave across his high forehead. She knew he was good-looking, certainly, but his gaze seemed to pierce her being and make her feel naked and vulnerable.

She quivered with longing and desire when Robert touched her. A moan escaped involuntarily through her pursed lips. She locked her arms around his muscular neck, drawing his taut body closer for a kiss, and she heard him whisper, "Give me the true essence of your femininity." She knew she mustn't, but she couldn't lose him now.

"That's pretty good," I said. Can I read it when you're done?"

"You're joking, right?"

"Yes."

"Most of our books are serious, about sisters and daughters and mothers, but this is what Pam likes."

"She might enjoy historical, small-town, reverse-harem or contemporary, enemies-to-lovers, single-dad, billionaire romance."

"I'll let her know."

"Is Pam married?"

"Divorced."

"She should get re-married. That might satiate her interest in romantic longing and desire."

"I don't think so," Katya said.

I considered that.

"By the way," Katya said. "I saw Sean at school. He's back supply teaching."

"I know. He told me. There can't be many paying guests in his B and B during the school year."

"He might know Tyson as well."

"I should ask him," I said.

"Sean gets a good pension. He's probably bored, and I think he genuinely cares about the kids," Katya said and returned to her book.

Chapter 10

Work is a great way to kill time, which is fine when you're young and have lots. I felt like I might be beginning to run out and should ration it. I believe that as one begins to run out of time, it runs faster toward the finish line. The week was filled with work interrupted by meals, trips to the gym and sleeps, none of which I remembered clearly. I decided to pay Sean a visit after work, after a trip to the gym, but before my next sleep to change things up.

My car knew the way to the Coventry Recreational Complex. When I arrived, I saw a sign saying that all the swim lanes were closed for a week of maintenance. I scanned my card at the check-in desk and walked across the hall to peek through the gallery window at blue-painted concrete. When they filled the pool up again, the water would be freezing.

I changed into gym clothes, shoved my stuff into a locker and headed to the weight room. A middle-aged man with a familiar, paunchy profile was checking what looked like a cue card for body parts that he was supposed to exercise that day. I went over for a closer look.

"Hey Jackson. Are you getting bored with retirement yet?" I asked.

"Yes. Hi Matt."

"You working on your quads, squats, lats or abs today?"

"What's your advice? You're in great shape."

"My advice is exercise whatever part feels like it has excess energy."

"If I did that, I would have to just go home," Jackson said.

"How are you filling up your days?"

"I'm teaching criminology at the community college, Matt. I could see there wasn't going to be much chauffeuring work when you rode away from my place on a bicycle."

"I'm back to driving again. I had a flat tire that day. My paranoid personality tells me my SUV was vandalized."

"I saw your vehicle parked outside Gleeson Court across from a police cruiser the other day."

"Yes, that time it was personal. One of the residents stole my cell phone from our hockey change room."

"Who was it? I know most of the yahoos in there," Jackson said in a cop voice.

"Does the name Gruber ring a bell?"

"Sure. I know old Zeke all right. He's been up on charges before."

"Not Zeke, Tyson."

"No. I don't think so. Could there be two of them?"

"Tyson is only a teenager. Zeke could be his runaway dad. Maybe a fugitive from justice," I said.

"Gruber is a common name in this area. Well, at least you got your phone back." Jackson was eyeing the iPhone clipped to my belt. "What happened to the old burner flip-phone? You used to say you didn't want balls cancer or the CIA always knowing where you were."

I shifted the device farther away from my balls. "I didn't know I needed it until I got one."

"Hey, how about giving a lecture on coronering at my course?"

"What's the pay?"

"The same as for coroner chauffeuring. There's no budget."

"I have stage fright."

"What about as a favour?" He was making it hard for me to refuse.

"I guess I could use it toward my quota of continuing medical education hours," I said. "We have to do a certain number every year."

"That's the spirit. I'll email you some possible dates then?"

"Okay. Maybe I could do a Q and A so there would be less preparation. What kind of profession does this course lead to?"

"Most of them apply to become cops or paralegals."

"Okay."

"Can you come next Tuesday evening at 7 o'clock?"

"Okay." I was sorry I had gone over to talk to him.

Sean lived on a one-way residential street, so after driving across town, I had to go around a block of nineteenth-century stately homes to get to his two-story bed and breakfast hotel. He was out trimming hedges when I pulled up. I hadn't seen him since our train trip to Toronto.

"Matthew!" he called and waved.

I stopped the car and rolled down the window.

Sean was burly with a steel-grey brush cut and grey eyebrows, which, like his hedges, were perfectly trimmed to an even length. He walked over in his gardening boots. "Well, it's good to see you, Matthew."

I didn't need any more of an invitation to get out of the car. "Thanks Sean. I see you're keeping yourself busy."

"I'm also playing golf three times a week and back at school twice a week as a guidance counsellor."

He had to be busy. Before golf, Sean had owned a sailboat in which he and his wife had crossed the Atlantic. He sold it after Sinead refused to ever board it again.

"Katya mentioned you had gone back to teaching. What provoked that? Did you experience an existential crisis?"

"It helps pay for grass seed. Those little bastards do need guidance though. There are some very sad, hard-luck stories out there. Kids living with single parents with drug or alcohol addiction—sometimes no parents. I had one like that yesterday."

"Was his name Tyson Gruber?"

"How could you have known that, Matthew?"

"I was a witness to his apprehension by the long arm of the law while he was carrying a bag of cell phones."

"Was your phone in that bag?"

"Yep."

"First his mother, then his father deserted him, and he's only 15-years-old. He's in foster care now, but who really wants a 15-year-old who's up on charges in their home. He smokes like a chimney, but he's not a druggie. He's well-spoken and has a good heart. I would say reformable."

"What's going to happen with the criminal charges?"

"It's his first offence and he's underage. He'll probably get probation for theft under $5000."

"My phone was worth $1500. There were five phones missing."

"Have a heart, Matthew. He's not a hard-core criminal yet. I actually organized a co-op work term for him. He'll be helping me redo the plumbing and install ensuite bathrooms for the two guest rooms that don't have them yet."

"If he was short of money, he could have gotten a job flipping burgers at MacDonald's instead of stealing my phone."

"I'm paying him now… He was trying to avoid foster care. The rent was due. He needed money to pay the rent, and he doesn't like to miss school… I'm serious."

"You must have really hit it off with Tyson."

"He's a victim of circumstances who needs a break. He told me his mother was born in Ireland."

"More like a con-man preying on your good nature. Does anyone know where his parents are?"

"His father sold drugs and his mother was a user. They weren't together very long. She might be dead of an overdose somewhere. He's probably on the run from the police, or his suppliers if he crossed them."

"Isn't Gruber a Mennonite name? That doesn't sound very Christian."

"There's a Mennonite drug pipeline from Mexico. Ask your cop friends."

"That reminds me I have to talk to Detective Branko Marcovic. You've met him, I think."

"I met him before he made detective when I caught some little bastard breaking into my garage at night." Sean picked up a rake from the grass to gather the hedge clippings. "I kept him cornered with the blunt end of this." He smiled as if in fond remembrance.

"Couldn't you reform that one?"

Sean's wife Sinead came out to join us. She was tall with dark hair and freckles. Her steps were measured and graceful.

"Hello Matthew. How are you?" Her lilt betrayed that, like Sean, she was born in Ireland.

"I'm very well thanks."

"I just saw Katya at movie club, Matthew."

"Of course, you see Katya all the time in your clubs. I don't get invited so I don't get to see you as often as I'd like."

"It's just girl talk. You aren't missing anything. Dinner's ready. Can you stay for dinner, Matthew?"

"Katya texted she was making something and it sounded pretty yummy. Let's do a proper dinner together, on the weekend maybe."

"I'd love to do that, Matthew."

"Will you and Katya have anything left to talk about?"

"Women are never short of conversation, and it's interesting even if you've heard it before."

"What about all these clubs that exclude men? Are you in favour of that?"

"Well, that's sort of the point isn't it, Matthew?"

"That's what Katya said."

Although I hadn't really gotten a text from Katya, she was just putting the finishing touches on dinner when I walked in. It was lucky I hadn't accepted Sinead's offer. There was beet soup with sour cream and dill, followed by breaded schnitzel with lemon wedges and dill, buttermilk mashed potatoes with dill, and sauerkraut— Polish standards that Katya had learned from her mother.

"This looks and smells great," I said. "What's the occasion?"

"I just felt like cooking. It's Polish Constitution Day."

I loaded up my plate, took out my phone and snapped a picture. "I'm going to send this to Harper so she knows what to cook to get Michael to marry her. Her biological clock is ticking."

"Don't do it."

"And dab a little sauerkraut juice behind your ears tonight if you want to get lucky."

As we were finishing dinner, I heard a noise I disliked coming from near my waistline.

"What's that? It sounds like hoarse crickets," Katya said.

"It's just called *Crickets*. It provokes less shell-shocked startle response. My phone is ringing."

I wasn't on call, but sometimes the hospital called when they needed a second anesthesiologist, when the anesthesiologist on call was already involved in a case. It happened most often with emergency Caesarean sections, or because a surgeon was getting petulant about having to wait. Dolly's name was on the call display.

Dolly lived in the house diagonally across the street from where I grew up in Scarborough. She might have been 15 years older than me. I hadn't spoken to her in about a year because the last time she called a few months before, I had let it go to voicemail and never called back. I hesitated and then picked up.

"Hi Dolly. How are you?"

"Hi Matt. Are you busy? Do you have a minute to talk?"

"I have a few minutes, Dolly." I walked into my study and took a seat. This was going to take a while.

"I hate to bother you. Today is the anniversary of Francis' death and I was feeling kind of low. It was a lot of years ago, but you really never get over it. You remember him, don't you, Matt?"

"It's no bother, Dolly. I remember him. Francis died too young."

"Frank had a heart attack when he was only 62. He had the bypass and stenting after that and took his retirement from the post office. It might have bought him a few extra years. We were watching TV together, and he said he was feeling some tightness so I went to the kitchen to get his nitroglycerine, and when I got back he was gone. We got married when we were only 18. I didn't know any other life without him.

"I remember you as a cute little kid. I remember the time you sat on the curb in front of my house and you wouldn't go home because you thought you would get a spanking for throwing a rock at Wayney. I told you your mum said she wouldn't spank you if you went home. Didn't you hit him in the head with a rock, Matt?"

"It was a piece of gravel and I was returning fire. It was a lucky shot from a distance. I got the spanking anyway."

"It's comforting to hear you talk about the old days, Matt. Tell me more about your life since you left Scarborough."

I hated this type of open-ended question. It meant she was settling in for a nice long chat. I didn't really owe her that. We weren't related. It was an accident of geography that we knew each other.

"I work a lot, Dolly. I am an anesthesiologist three or four days a week. I work in an operating room. It's like working in a factory. We do six or seven different operations in a day, but the anesthetics are almost the same every time. The surgeons get worked up over increasing efficiency and rapid turnover to make more money."

"Are they on your case about it, Matt?"

"Sure they are. I try not to hold them up, but I won't let them rush me into cutting corners. I also work as a coroner—you know, helping the police decide on a cause of death."

"That sounds interesting, Matt. You must have to look at some really nasty things, like gun shot wounds and rotten corpses."

"There is some of that. The typical case is an old person who dies at home who has no doctor to fill out a death certificate. The cops call me for that all the time."

I reflected that maybe I was hitting too close to home. Dolly might fit that description some day soon.

"Wayney Delaney was a funny one," she said. "They say he was a biker faggot, but I don't care about that. He had no right to run into your SUV with his motorcycle. It's like he had a grudge against you. Do ya think it was an accident, Matt?"

"I think it was suicide."

"Well, isn't that the darndest thing. Suicide. Like suicide by cop, only suicide by doctor. Was there some bad blood between you growing up?

"Dolly, it's complicated. He thought I had something to do with his best friend's death in Coventry."

"Did ya kill him, Matt? Was he a biker too?"

"No. I knew him. He was hitting on my wife, but I didn't kill him. Wayney was living in a fantasy world." It seemed weird discussing this with Dolly. Whether I was or was not responsible for James Basciuseson's death was not something I cared to share with her. Other than myself, Sean and Jeremiah Chang were the only people alive who knew the answer to that. It was time to change the subject and then hang up. "How do you fill your days, Dolly?"

"I cut the grass just before I called you. We've got an old push mower. I could get a power mower but there isn't a lot of grass and it gives me some exercise. I watch my programs in the evening. Most of the people on the street are younger couples now, mostly immigrants, so they don't want nothing to do with me."

"Well, there were a lot of immigrants on our street before too. My family immigrated from Eastern Europe."

"Yes. We were all young, so it didn't seem to matter. I walk to the top of the street to get a pizza or some Chinese. I still know some of the people in the stores."

"You never had children, did you Dolly? Do you have sisters or brothers close by?"

"I had a couple of miscarriages. Frank was so disappointed."

After thirty more minutes of this, I said, "Okay Dolly. I'm going to have to let you go. I've got a work call coming through on my phone." This was a lie of course.

"Okay Matt. Thank you for taking the time. I'm all alone now."

"You're welcome, Dolly. I'm sorry about Francis. Let's talk again in a few months."

"Sorry, Matt. People like me talk about their constipation and their pills. It's all new to them. They've never been old before."

"It's good to hear from you, Dolly."

I came back into the kitchen and saw that as well as having done all the cooking, Katya had already done most of the cleanup. That, theoretically, was my job if she had cooked.

"Who was that?" Katya asked.

"Dolly, from Scarborough. I told you about her. I have to change my phone number."

Chapter 11

Huronia Community College was located in a converted high school in the industrial area of Coventry. There was no welcome person or posting of room numbers for courses in the entrance foyer. I found the classroom where Jackson taught criminology by wandering the hallways past lockers and water fountains and peeking in doorways until I recognized him.

Jackson beckoned me in when he saw me. "Hey Matt. Glad you could make it."

"Hi Jackson. Sorry I'm late. Would it be okay if I talk until I run out of ideas and then open it up for questions? I don't have any slides."

"Yeah, sure. Your talk, your rules. They might have stomachs too sensitive for slides anyway."

There were about twenty students sitting in pairs on old fashioned stacking chairs at wooden tables etched with decades of carved initials. There was an equal mix of guys and girls aged about twenty to thirty. Jackson warmed up the audience for me with some anecdotes and introduced me as their special guest. They had notepads, textbooks, laptops and cups of coffee, just like a real class.

I told them the difference between the coronial system, where regular doctors do scene visits and decide on the cause of death, and the medical examiner system, where centrally located pathologists direct a team of paramedical personnel who bring bodies to them. Medical examiners view scene photographs, decide whether to do autopsies and then *they* assign the cause of death.

I told them about the difference between cause and manner of death. Cause means medical cause. The five manners are natural, accident, suicide, homicide, with murder being a subtype of homicide as defined by law, and undetermined. Non-natural deaths could be sub-classified by mechanism as blunt force, sharp force, asphyxial or environmental. Victims are generally beaten, shot, stabbed or strangled, unless they are suffocated, frozen or poisoned.

The medical examiner system exists in some Canadian provinces and in many U.S. states. Medical examiners are pathologists, so they never see live patients. They specialize in doing autopsies, so there are more autopsies in that system. An autopsy usually involves dissection, or it could be virtual, where they pass the body through a CT scanner. Since coroners are also community physicians, they would look up and interpret online medical records, talk to witnesses and relatives and decide the cause of death with fewer autopsies.

In Britain, coroners are lawyers, so they have more inquests. Inquests are quasi-legal proceedings with a judge and lawyers who elicit testimony from witnesses. Based on this, they determine a cause of death and make recommendations. Each different type of professional does what they know best. I opened the talk up to questions.

A young man put up his hand, which I acknowledged. "So, like, do you put cosmetics on a dead body?"

"No, that's an undertaker, also known as a funeral director."

Another person raised their hand. "So, then you cut the body open, right?"

"No. That's a pathologist."

Someone called out, "So, do you put the chemicals in a dead body?"

"Undertaker again."

Another student asked, "So, what do *you* do?"

"Coroners in Ontario basically look at the body, any prescription or non-prescription drugs at the scene, the medical history on the provincial electronic database, talk to the relatives and decide whether an autopsy is required to determine the cause of death. We don't get called for every death—just suspicious cases, or if someone dies at home and there is no family doctor to do the paper work."

"Do you like it?"

"Not especially. I also do hospital work as an operating room anesthesiologist. If I just did that, I wouldn't get out much. Being a coroner might be a good retirement job after I finish my anesthesiology career. Coroner's cases can be interesting if they are unusual, and some of the police are nice. You can develop a camaraderie."

"How many murders have you seen?"

"Officially none, so far."

"Couldn't anyone do that coroner job if you have a medical examiner? On CSI, they have teams of people wearing coroner jackets, collecting evidence, stick a thermometer in the liver and then take the body to the medical examiner."

"We're not allowed to stick thermometers in the liver anymore. In Ontario right now, you have to be a doctor to be a coroner. The Ontario government is thinking of trying a medical examiner system to save money. A small number of pathologists would direct investigators, who could be ex-nurses, paramedics, undertakers, cops, whatever. Who's to say they're wrong?

"Doctors cost more, but more autopsies from a pathologist-run system and more inquests from a lawyer-run system would also cost more. I don't know what would be the cheapest. They have already hired some nurses to do natural causes deaths. They're called coroner-investigators. I'm an investigating coroner. The coroners here are trying to unionize to protect their jobs. It's been in the newspaper."

"What if someone accidentally kills another person? Is that a homicide or an accident? Like if a guy didn't know the rifle was loaded and then he shot someone in the head." I thought I recognized Piper, Taylor's friend from the Paul Simon concert. Was she pretending to know something about the Albert Yantzi case?

"Were you thinking of a specific incident, Piper?"

"No… Okay then, yeah. That case where Alec Baldwin, the actor, killed another actor with what he thought was an unloaded pistol when they were making a movie."

"I would call that an accident although technically it is a homicide as well. The decision requires an inference about mental state. There is no category for accidental homicide. Piper, could you stay after class for a minute to speak with me?"

She reluctantly nodded her head.

"What if someone starves themselves to death in jail as a protest. Is that suicide?" someone else asked.

"I would think so, yes."

"What if they had anorexia nervosa?"

"Then the manner of death would be natural because they had a mental illness. Okay, that's it. Talk's over."

There was a polite round of applause. Jackson gave them a homework assignment from their textbook for next week and said see you at the same time in six days and 23 hours. Piper filed past me on her way out.

"Hi Piper. You want to become a crime scene investigator?"

"Sure, why not. It's better than a life of crime." She seemed uncomfortable at my remembering her name.

"Welcome to the club. Don't steal my job. How are Taylor and Parker doing?"

"Taylor's busy cleaning out her father's apartment. Parker is looking after her little kid. She doesn't have a lot of money. They are hoping you hurry up and do the right thing."

"I always try to do the right thing."

"I could tell you a few things, but I won't."

"About what, Piper?"

She smiled and filed past. I decided not to press the issue.

Jackson walked out with me when everyone else had left. He looked pleased with how the hour had gone.

"Thanks a lot, Matt. I think they enjoyed that. It answered a lot of questions for me too."

"You're welcome, Jackson."

"I didn't know you were trying to unionize."

"Trying is right. There is an outright physician exemption to unionization in the Labour Relations Act. It specifically excludes lawyers, doctors, dentists and land surveyors."

"Land surveyors?"

"Land surveyors are excluded but not teachers, cops or crown attorneys."

"Why no more meat thermometers?"

"They say that the rate of post-mortem cooling is too variable. I suspect that they also don't want us to gross out relatives who might be watching."

"That's hilarious—coroner-investigators and investigating coroners. So, I read in the newspaper that they're trying to get homeless people to do your job. Any truth to that?"

"You owe me a case of beer."

When I got home, I found Katya sitting in the kitchen with the morning newspaper spread out on the kitchen counter, open at the crossword. She had saved it for a bedtime treat. "What's another word for military attaché? Your father was military."

"Why don't you cheat and ask Google?" I suggested.

"That's a last resort."

"Isn't it cheating if I tell you?"

"We're a team, hon."

"Adjutant."

"That fits. Thanks! Michael and Harper are coming home for dinner tomorrow night." Harper was my son Michael's girlfriend.

"That's good, but what about your colonoscopy. It's in two days. Shouldn't you be starting to fast?"

"I cancelled that weeks ago," Katya said. "You said it would be okay because the surgeon hadn't seen me yet."

"Well, hopefully, Chandler won't even know you were booked to see him. Did his secretary know who you were when you called to cancel?"

"No, I don't think so. She didn't say anything. Can you get me an appointment with someone else?"

"Yes. It might save embarrassment if you went out of town. I'll ask around to find out who's good in Somerset."

"Michael can finally install the hard-drives when he comes," Katya said.

I had ordered two large hard-drives to automatically back up the contents of our home computers. Michael had told me which ones to buy and texted me that he could install them when he visited next. I was careful to leave them untouched in their original packaging. He took pleasure in evaluating every component of new electronics, beginning with slowly removing the packaging, like a striptease.

Michael and Harper arrived together in a car-share rental vehicle the following evening. They had been a couple since high school. Katya hugged them both while I fist-bumped with them. I didn't want Harper to think I was a lecher. I couldn't hug Michael without hugging Harper.

Michael had a degree in software engineering and was working on his master's degree in computer science. A lot of people asked Michael for help with their computers. His stock answer was something like, "Computers are hard." This meant no. He and his classmates had T-shirts with the logo, *No I won't fix your computer*. I paid him a tax-deductible monthly salary from which he paid his university tuition, so he couldn't refuse me.

After preliminary greetings, we gathered at the dinner table.

"How is the work on your Masters going?" I asked Michael.

"Good."

"Tell me again what you're working on. Someone was asking me."

"How much detail do you want?"

"Just give me the escalator pitch, so I can remember it."

"I'm working on algorithms for compressing images and videos without losing detail by inferring details. Streaming services could save bandwidth but the average user would also save space on his phone or computer."

"His or her," Harper corrected.

"His or her," Michael agreed. "What about you? Have you had any good coroner cases lately?"

"I went to one where the body was so badly decomposed that I had to wear a hazmat suit from the fire department. How much detail do you want?"

"How did he die?"

"It might have been a suicide. The estranged daughter is trying to get me to fill out papers for life insurance. She won't be able to collect if it's a suicide, which it looks like it is."

"Was this in Coventry?" Harper asked.

"Yes. Not too far from here. The funny thing was that I ran into the daughter in Toronto with her friends Piper and Parker." The names had stuck because they were both occupations and they alliterated.

"I know Piper and Parker," Harper said. "Parker was hooked up with some old dude. He could have been almost your age. In our last year of high school, he would be smoking a cigarette just off the school property, waiting for her."

"Do you remember his name?"

"It was Taylor Yantzi's father."

"Are you effing kidding me?"

"No. That's who everyone said it was," Harper said defensively.

"Did you know those people, Michael?"

"No, but I know more about computers than people."

"Are they related? Was Albert Yantzi her guardian?" I asked.

"No." Harper said. "She has her own parents. They were hooked up, I told you. Parker was getting drugs from him."

"The plot thickens. Thanks for telling me, Harper, and forget I told you about Piper and Parker. I'm not supposed to gossip."

"Okay."

I didn't know whether this meant that Taylor and Parker were somehow allied in trying to collect on Albert's life insurance. It seemed from what Piper had said that they might be. Parker would almost certainly have no rights as a beneficiary, unless Albert specifically had included her as one.

While we were talking, the landline rang. I didn't have time to banter with scammers or charities. The call display showed our local area code. I picked up and mentally settled on saying, "Would you happen to have a giant rubber dildo in the call centre?"

"Can you come over to the house after work tomorrow, Matt?" It was Sean Feeney.

"I guess so. Are you inviting me for dinner?"

"Yes. Just you. Katya's not invited."

"Why not? She likes to eat dinner."

"Come to think of it, I need her also for his accounting homework. This is a working dinner though. I want you to help Tyson Gruber with a biology paper he's done. It's not my area. I want you to read it through before he submits it. You're stronger than I am in maths and sciences."

"I don't think I owe him anything."

"Think of it as your good deed for the year. It might not be too late to turn him around."

"You're far more community-minded than I am."

"It's important to me that we try, Matt."

"No problem then, Sean. What time?"

"See you around six."

After dessert, I stacked the boxed hard drives on the kitchen table in front of Michael, knowing that he couldn't resist. Katya entertained Harper while Michael pored over the boxes. After he slowly undressed the electronics from their packaging, he lovingly read the technical manuals and researched and tested every potential issue. He didn't leave until 11 p.m. when Harper finally dragged him out the door.

Chapter 12

I checked the weather on my phone. The forecast was for sunny and cool. I love sunny and cool, but it was a waste because I had to work. I brought up the hospital Covid screening questionnaire. Although the pandemic was nearly over, we weren't allowed to enter the building without completing it.

Agreeing that I had no unexplained fever, malaise, rhinorrhea or cough, had not travelled and had been vaccinated many more times than twice meant that I could enter through the side entrance and avoid the human screeners. The questionnaire was window dressing. I suspected that at this stage of the pandemic the unspoken agenda was just to let everyone get Covid. Vaccinations ameliorated but did not prevent it, and the disease was less lethal for everyone except the elderly. For economic reasons, this dry tinder could burn where it may.

Katya was in the kitchen ahead of me, leisurely leafing through the newspaper.

"Can't sleep?" I asked.

"No."

"Not working today?"

"No. I'm playing golf today at 10 a.m. It's nice enough to play again."

"Play hard. Hit a home run. Don't take any shit from anyone."

My cell phone rang. Only my wife, the hospital, the cops, Dolly and the Coroners' Answering Service had the number. I was due in the O.R., so I couldn't accept any coroner's cases. I ignored the call and rushed out the door. If it was the hospital, they would see me soon enough.

There was a list of D&Cs and hysterectomies for Adam to do. A D&C, or dilatation and curettage, is a procedure where the inside lining of the uterus is scraped with a curette. It's done in women with post-menopausal bleeding to look for cancer. It's also done to remove remnants of a miscarriage to allow the uterus to contract and stop bleeding. It is a very common procedure as about 15 per cent of pregnancies end in miscarriages.

We brought the first young lady who was having a D&C into the operating room and got her settled on the O.R. table. I gave her some fentanyl and a bolus of intravenous fluids while Sara administered oxygen through the anesthesia mask.

The patient seemed more than usually anxious. Sara was following her head around with the oxygen mask as it shifted. She said, "When I move my head, everything goes wonky."

"Don't move your head then," Sara said.

I gave the first drugs in the induction sequence.

"I know that, but..." and then she passed out.

"Why do you think drugs would make you feel wonky?" Sara asked.

"We don't really understand drugs," I said.

Sara and Adam positioned the patient's legs up in stirrups.

"Hey, did you ever get paid for that Mennonite Caesarean section?" I asked Adam. "I think their name was Yantzi."

"I don't know. Call my secretary. She could look it up."

"You just do this as a public service?"

"My head's too full to think about that. I just know I am doing the Lord's work helping people any way I can." Adam's eyes indicated that he was smiling behind his mask.

"That's very patient-centred of you," Sara said.

"It's hard though, mon. The hospital keeps doing more shite. For instance, this flippin' new dictation system. Yesterday, I dictated a patient's history, 'Seizures and Parkinson's disease,' and transcribed on de fucking screen was, "She has ears and Parking Still Indian's disease."

Our new automated transcription system saved money on human typists.

"I see your point," I said. "Did you fix it?"

"Of course I fixed it! I typed it all out manually. Do ya tink I want some fucking lawyer readin' dat? If I left it, I may as well sign it 'please sue my ass.' " His tone was getting shrill. Obstetrics and gynecology was the most highly sued specialty.

After a few minutes of silence, he said, "You'll get your money, mon. Mennonites almost always pay. They got some of my money yesterday at a Mennonite roadside stand. There was a little kid behind it selling vegetables. I asked him where your parents at and he said, 'They got the Covid.' "

"Mrs. Yantzi's husband is also involved in one of my coroner cases."

"Then he'll pay you in Covid pickles and Covid sweet corn. Coroners take corn currency, right?"

Adam was taking longer than usual with his uterine scraping and free associating. I thought it might be because I was distracting him, so I stopped talking and glanced at the list of emails on my phone. There was a notification that a final pathology report had been uploaded onto the coroners' secure website. It would take a series of passwords to open and look at it.

"I'm having a little trouble. Can someone pull up YouTube surgery?" Adam said from between the patient's legs. My next thought was that he had accidentally perforated the uterus. I turned down the anesthetic gas and started pumping intravenous fluids.

Two minutes later, Adam said, "Okay, I'm …" I didn't catch what he said he was.

"The from-between-the legs-acoustics-aren't great. Did you say you were done?"

"Ya-mon. Did you think I said I had perforated the uterus?"

"No." It is generally true in the practice of anesthesia that you will have fewer regrets if you always prepare for the worst.

Adam, Sara and I worked as a team to slide the patient off the operating table onto her stretcher. As she was moving, the patient's gown shifted revealing her breasts. I sometimes wondered whether Sara arranged for this to happen to see my response. It seemed to happen more often than could be expected strictly by chance when we worked together. I quickly pulled the patient's gown back up to cover her chest.

"As long as your areola is covered, you're not naked," Sara said.

The caller from the morning phoned again when I broke for lunch. There weren't enough digits in the call display to be a scammer, so I picked up.

"Hi. It's Taylor McGuire. I'm so sorry to bother you."

"How did you get my number, Taylor?"

"I called the hospital to get your number to get a copy of my father's death certificate, but they wouldn't give it to me. The police suggested I call the funeral home, Christobel's, where my father was cremated, and their secretary gave me your number. They didn't have a copy of the death certificate either."

Some of the funeral homes had my number too. I hadn't remembered that. They texted me to expedite cremation certificates to move bodies to the crematorium to make space for new ones. "I didn't issue the death certificate yet, Taylor," I said. "The manner of death is still officially undetermined."

"But how could he have been cremated without a death certificate? The insurance company says that's what I need and to get it from you."

"I issued a Warrant to Bury, which covers cremations. Taylor, the girl I saw you with in Toronto… I think her name was Parker."

"Yes," she said nervously.

"Was she your father Albert's girlfriend?"

"Yes."

"How is that possible? When did she last see him alive?"

"It's the reason I haven't spoken to my father in over ten years. He was having sex with my best friend—my very own father."

"Was she still carrying on the relationship with your dad before he died?"

"Not for a few years, but sometimes before that. He would give her money and drugs. She told me she stopped seeing him when she got a boyfriend. She told me she doesn't do drugs anymore—that much."

"Did your father molest you, Taylor?"

"No. Never. That's not the reason I went away. I lived half-time with him and half-time with my mom until I turned 18, and then I moved to Toronto and got a job and never spoke with him again."

"When did Parker last see your father?"

"A few weeks before he died, I guess."

I paused to digest that. Parker was the girlfriend who had notified Albert's superintendent. "Okay, thanks for telling me. I issued a Warrant to Bury. It doesn't require a cause of death to be filled in. It means we've finished examining the body, and the relatives can have it back for cremation or burial. The toxicology testing showed hydromorphone, a narcotic, and flubromazolam, a benzodiazepine tranquilizer. I expect to get the final pathologist's report shortly."

"Okay."

"Taylor, your half-brother Caleb wrote me saying that he thinks your father was murdered. The police are still up in the air as to whether the death was a suicide or a homicide. We'll form a final determination soon after I get the pathologist's final report and the police investigation is finished. I'll call you then."

"Okay."

"Taylor, do you know whether Caleb is also a beneficiary to your father's insurance policy?"

"Yes."

"He is?"

"Yes."

"Do you have any questions?"

"No."

"Okay then, goodbye Taylor. I'll call you when the final report is available."

I drove over to Sean's house after work. Sean and Tyson were in the shed behind the house, organizing some plumbing hardware.

Tyson looked different from the way I remembered. He was dressed in jeans, a button-down collar shirt and a leather jacket with the cuffs rolled up. His yellow hair was cut and styled. His square jaw was clean-shaven and he was smiling. Aside from being too skinny, he had natural David-Bowie-style good looks.

Sean said, "Tyson has something to say to you, Matt."

"Hey Dr. Kork, I'm sorry I stole your phone." He took a drag of his cigarette and smiled again, waiting for absolution.

I waited for more.

"My dad buggered off. I fell in with some bad company—a guy who could fence cell phones. I needed cash in a hurry to keep living in my apartment. That's not who I am though."

Now he was waiting. It seemed sincere, but I didn't detect any note of remorse. Sean didn't say anything.

"I've never had to face circumstances as tough as yours, Tyson. I guess I don't know what I would have done in your place."

Tyson held out his hand confidently. I took it and he gripped it, grinning widely at me.

"I understand you want me to proof-read a paper you've done."

"Yes please."

We went in for dinner. There were several steaming casserole dishes on the kitchen table. The four of us took our seats around it.

"Welcome again, Matthew," Sinead said. "We decided, why wait for the weekend to have the pleasure of your company for dinner. Help yourselves everyone."

Sean extended both his arms. This was something new. We all linked hands while Sean said grace, after which he gave me a surreptitious glance. Sean taught in a Catholic school, but only put the existence of God at 50-50. Sinead barely ate, but the three men more than made up for that. They kept pressing more food on Tyson, which he happily accepted. I had the feeling that he could have eaten even more.

After dinner, Tyson and I moved to the dining room and he spread his work out on the large table. He had written a biology paper, which I skimmed, making corrections in the margins with a pencil. He had chosen to write about the pharmacology of street drugs. We also reviewed the most recent chapters from his mathematics textbook. His math skills were about two years behind what was in the book. After an hour he suggested a coffee break.

"I can't drink coffee this late," I said.

"I drink at least six cups a day," Tyson said. "It doesn't affect me."

He made a cupful of instant in the kitchen and we went outside so that he could smoke.

"Sean seems to have taken a personal interest in you," I said.

"Mr. Feeney is a good head. He's one of the good ones." He held his cigarette in his palm between his thumb and index finger, flicking ashes with his ring finger.

"He's seen a lot of the world. He can teach you a lot. He might see something of himself in you. Did you normally say grace before meals at home?"

"I do that religious stuff with Mr. Feeney because he seems to like it."

"You're not going to let him down are you, Tyson?"

"No way. I would never do that."

"Do you do drugs, Tyson?" I was wondering about his choice of biology project.

"I hate drugs. The worst I've done is smoke a little weed. My mother overdosed."

"I'm sorry. Was it accidental?"

"She had depression. I found her lying on her bed when I got home from school. She'd dressed up and done her hair. I guess she wanted to look nice when I found her. There were old photographs of me she'd propped up against the lamp on the night stand, and empty pill bottles."

"That's tragic… Is your father's name Zeke?"

"Yes."

"Has he been in touch with you?"

"He sent me a text after he left. It said that he had to disappear for a while. There were some guys who were after him."

"Have you heard anything since?"

"No… I'm going to finish high school so I can learn a trade. I'm interested in plumbing or electrical. You need high school math to qualify for an apprenticeship. Electrical work is cleaner than plumbing, but then there is the risk of getting accidentally shocked."

"You've thought this through."

"Yes I have."

"An apprenticeship is five years, isn't it?"

"Yes."

"You know your way around hockey arenas. Do you play, Tyson?"

"I play net in a pick-up league Tuesday nights. I'm also a rent-a-goalie for forty bucks when a team is short."

"The doctors' team sometimes needs a goalie. Are you interested?"

"Well, I ripped off their phones. How would they feel about that?"

"Maybe it's too soon. I'll ask them next season."

"Okay. I'm done my break," Tyson said. "Can we get back to work? I have to get that math sorted out before my test on Friday. That apprenticeship isn't going to happen by itself."

We went back inside and I tried to catch him up on some basic concepts in math that he had missed. We worked until 10 p.m. when Sean re-appeared to drive Tyson back to his foster-home. I didn't trust him entirely, but I was impressed by his optimism in the face of adversity. He seemed, at the core, possibly, to be a nice kid.

Chapter 13

The final pathology report that I had been alerted to by email had been uploaded to the coroners' secure website. I brought it up on my computer at home the next morning. I was first prompted to change my password. It was a pain in the ass to keep track of what password was current on a page full of used and crossed out passwords and then think of a new one. The password was followed by a second-factor identification from my cell phone. The report belonged to Albert Yantzi.

I scrolled to the last page of the ten-page document to read the conclusions before reading through the minutiae. Under the heading, CAUSE of DEATH, was written:

Acting on the authority of a Coroner's Warrant for Postmortem Examination, I hereby certify that I have examined this body, opened and examined the cavities, organs and tissues as indicated, and based on my findings and information made available to me, in my opinion the cause of death was:

Part 1
Immediate cause of death: Gunshot wound to the head.

MAJOR FINDINGS
Low-velocity, intermediate-range gunshot wound left external auditory canal
a) multiple comminuted fractures of calvarium and base of skull
b) expulsion of left orbital contents
c) deformed bullet fragments retrieved from both cerebral hemispheres
c) toxicology positive for hydromorphone and flubromazolam, qualitative results only

Ronald J. Rasmussen MD, FRCPC
Pathologist

The preceding pages described the appearance and weight of every organ. There were no other significant abnormalities found and no mention of mesh for a hernia repair. The final pathology report contained no information additional to the preliminary. However, I wasn't allowed to submit my final report until I had received it.

The pathologist had left the manner of death for me to decide. This was of course appropriate, but I was reluctant to decide on my own. It was time for a case conference with the pathologist and Regional Supervising Coroner to get their input and spread the responsibility. I emailed Richard Tull to ask him whether it would be possible to organize this.

I went into the kitchen and found Katya on her usual perch, sitting on a stool by the counter, doing the newspaper crossword. The landline was ringing, which she was ignoring. I leaned over to look at the call display. It showed a local area code, but the phone number was typed twice on the screen. I put it on speakerphone.

After a fifteen-second period of silence, a voice said, "Hello, this is JK Duct Cleaning. We would like to come to your house to clean your ducts."

"My ducts are already clean."

"No sir. They are not clean. When did you clean them sir the last time?"

"They swim in the pond out back every day."

"No sir. We will clean the ducts inside your house."

"Well okay," I said. "Come over, but we're only eating one tonight."

"No sir. I mean your own ducts in your house."

"Oh, I see. Mine are clean too. I shot my load up into the wife this morning. Cleaned them out good. The wife's ducts could be bunged up now. I'll ask her."

"No sir, for your house furnace and air conditioning."

"Katya, there's a man on the phone who wants to talk to you."

"Hello. This is Mrs. Judy Heinbuch," she said. "I think Glen shot that spunk up too high and I'm afraid I'm gonna get bunged up again. When can you come over to the house? How far are you?"

"JK is very close to your house in Canada, Madame."

"May I call you JK?"

"Yes Madame."

"Our address is 34554345 County Road 7, Rural Route 42, Pickleburg, Ontario. Now, that's just a little bit north of Wartburg."

"We need a small deposit on your credit card, Madame. Do your have your VISA card ready?"

"Now, you just get on the airplane. We can sort that all out when you get here. I'm guessing it would be the same distance flying either east or west. You can use your GPS when you land in Toronto, and you can stay for supper. Do you like roast duck?"

"Madame, I am vegetarian."

"See you tonight."

Katya hung up. "What's a vegetarian?" she asked me. "We don't have those in Poland. We should get rid of our landline. Only old people have those anymore."

"I can't. I need it for faxing coroner stuff—Authorities to Seize dental X-rays and hospital records."

"I guess you better go to the supermarket and see if they have any duck."

It was the night for Katya's book club. She didn't ever tell me I had to leave the house, but she did want me to make myself scarce. I had nowhere to go, so I left for the gym about ten minutes before the ladies were due to arrive at 7 p.m. I got back around 8:30 to find the driveway parked up with SUV's and minivans, obstructing the entrance to the garage.

I parked on the street behind the latecomers who couldn't get into the driveway. This left me free to go to any possible coroner calls. If I had been parked in the garage, I would have been barricaded in. Entering through the garage door, I heard the chatter of women and stopped to listen:

"Maryjane said she was feeling sick on the lift, and when we got to the top, it was all in cloud. Why didn't they call and re-schedule? Well, you know how fast the weather can change up there. The tour guide said anything you want from the concession stand is on me. Well, didn't she chow down on everything and then she was so sick. Well, she didn't throw up but she looked sick. I thought, well that's on you!"

There was a chorus of, "That's on her," and "That's right," and one dissenting, "Poor Maryjane."

I went down the hall to the living room and took up a pose at the entrance. "Hello ladies."

Half of them said, "Hi Matt," smiling expectantly, and the other half, having had their conversation interrupted, waited tolerantly for the intrusion to end.

"How many books could a book club book if a book club could book books?" I asked.

Nobody laughed. One of the attendees said, "one."

"We heard you had a flat tire, Matt," a woman I didn't recognize said.

"Yes. I got a man to fix it."

"We heard maybe it was vandalized. Do you know who might have done it?"

"I suspect no one. I suspect everyone."

"That's very Inspector Clouseau of you."

I flashed a smile to show there were no hard feelings about their having parked up my driveway and moved on to the kitchen to see what goodies they had brought. They normally did desert over their intermission. There was a variety of pastries, flans, lemon cakes, poppy seed cakes and a torte. Women prefer sweet, men prefer salty. I didn't think I would be within my rights to sample anything until they had had their right of first refusal. I knew from past experience that most of what I saw would become leftovers.

Retiring to my study, I found that Richard Tull had emailed me, giving me three potential dates and times for a case conference to assign a manner of death to Albert Yantzi. I was eager for closure and chose the earliest date, which was in two days.

It took place over landline phone on a three-way conference call. This was actually the most secure way of doing it. When he and Ron Rasmussen and I were gathered, Richard greeted us and then asked me to present the details of the case. I was a little surprised, as it clearly labelled me as third in the hierarchy. This was true, but I thought he might have been more subtle, and the details of the case were already familiar to everyone.

After a halting and somewhat disorganized start, I recited the history from my notes. Mr. Yantzi was discovered in his locked, second-floor apartment in an advanced state of decomposition and infestation with a vintage rifle by his side. He was last seen alive by his girlfriend three weeks before that. He may have been the father of this woman's young child. The autopsy identified the cause of death as a gunshot wound to the left side of the head but didn't fix the time of death any more closely than the time he was last seen alive.

"Did we consult the forensic entomologist to better ascertain the time of death, Matt or Ron?" Richard asked.

"No." Ron sounded defensive. "I didn't consider that. I probably didn't because after multiple insect life cycles she wouldn't know which generation of maggot she's looking at. It would be no more precise than the time last seen alive."

"We don't have an entomologist in Coventry, obviously," I said.

Ron amplified my description of the autopsy findings by saying that gunpowder tattooing made it a medium-range shot, from about six inches away. This distance and the entry wound in the ear made it less likely to be a suicide. His caveat was that Mr. Yantzi was not wearing shoes and therefore could have discharged the weapon with his foot. If this were true, then he might indeed have shot himself in the ear from six inches away.

"How do the police feel about it?" Richard asked.

"They're leaning toward suicide," I said. "They don't have any suspects."

"Was there a suicide note?" Richard asked hopefully.

"No." I said.

"Any psych history?"

"Not anywhere I could find," I said.

"He has a daughter, correct? Could she provide any insights about his mental health?"

"She's estranged. She didn't think he was suicidal."

"What about handedness, Matt?" Ron asked. "Were you able to find that out? He would have shot himself in the right side of the head if he was right-handed."

"The daughter said maybe left-handed. She wasn't sure. He has a son as well, but I've really only communicated with the daughter, who is next of kin. The police have interviewed the son."

Richard cleared his throat. "Well, until the police dig up more evidence, we'll have to say that the manner is undetermined. Is everyone in agreement?"

I heard myself and Ron Rasmussen say yes. I said that I would submit my final report that way and inform the police of the verdict.

I emailed Branko the details of our discussion and asked whether he had any input or questions. He replied thanks, and that doesn't leave us any further ahead, does it? It might have left Taylor Yantzi further ahead. I filled out the insurance documents she had given me citing the manner of death as undetermined. Taylor and the insurance adjustors would have to be satisfied with that.

It had been two months since Anna Yantzi's Caesarean section. The third notice that I sent to the Yantzis warned that I would refer their account to a collection agency if they didn't pay. The agency took a 50 per cent cut, but it was better than nothing. A week later, I got my bill back in the mail, with a one-line cryptic note scrawled at the bottom. It read, "How do you know I'm not going to pay?"

The implication seemed to be that he would pay if I found that his father's death was a homicide and he was able to collect on the insurance. That ship seemed to have sailed.

Chapter 14

I was on call at the hospital again. Every fourth night on call meant that I had been on call for about seven years of my life. I telephoned the coroners' answering service to tell them I wouldn't be available until the next morning when my call duties at the hospital were done.

We did a fractured hip at 9 a.m. with Joshua Smith followed by a D&C with Adam. As a precaution, I checked the equipment in the obstetric unit to make sure everything was ready for an emergency Caesarean section. There was nothing else on the operating list, so I drove home for lunch and a nap. I was always conscious of having to sleep in advance in case I got called through the night.

My nap was interrupted after half an hour by the jarring noise of my cell phone playing *By the Sea, By the Sea, By the Beautiful Sea*. It was Chandler. "I have a three-year-old boy with appendicitis, confirmed by ultrasound. Could we follow your next case with an appendectomy?"

"Okay, sure. I'm at home. There's nothing going on so we can do it now. When they bring him up to the O.R., please keep the parents with him until I get a chance to talk to them. I won't be able to take a history from a three-year-old."

Despite saying this, to whomever would listen, whenever I had a paediatric patient, things often got screwed up. The porter or the nurse who brought the patient up from the emergency department would leave the parents behind, and I would be confronted by a screaming three-year-old and everyone urging me to just get on with it.

"Okay, I'll tell them," Chandler said.

I staggered to the bathroom upstairs to brush my teeth and splash cold water on my face. Katya was busy making the bed and placing decorative pillows correctly. "Who was that on the phone?"

"Chandler Bing from Friends. He wants to do an appendectomy episode."

"Remember to take the 14th off—next Thursday."

"Why?"

"It's the day of my colonoscopy."

"You should have told me earlier. It's going to be tough now. I'll have to ask someone to switch days with me."

"Please Matthew. I need moral support."

"I could take you to work with me in the morning and check in on you through the day."

"No."

"Okay. No problem." I realized the hospital wasn't such a familiar place for her.

I texted Miller and he agreed within a few minutes. It was nice that his generation regarded responding to texts as an urgent obligation. I was glad I hadn't signed off my last message to him as a professor of puff-pastry and watery melons.

I went back to the operating room to change all the equipment over for a paediatric case. There is a surprising amount that needs to be done if the room was previously set up for an adult—different settings on the gas machine, a different anesthetic circuit, different intravenous tubing, age-appropriate laryngoscope, airways, syringes etcetera. It minimizes everyone's stress if everything is ready to go when a frightened, screaming child enters the room.

Having resolved to personally go down to emergency department to see the child before he could be separated from his parents, I headed off toward the elevator. I rounded the corner and recognized Parker, Taylor's friend from the concert, standing beside a hospital crib with high circumferential metal rails containing a small child. Chandler was as good as his word.

Parker Riordan was in her early thirties—slim, shoulder-length, streaky, dye-blonde hair, nice complexion, nicotine-stained fingers. She looked like she had been crying.

I picked up the chart from the end of the crib. "What's your son's name, Parker?" I asked.

"Oliver."

"You're Taylor's friend, aren't you? We met briefly in Toronto. Are you here alone with Oliver?"

"His dad's not in the picture anymore. Taylor was here with me today."

I wondered whether Albert Yantzi was the boy's father. I was curious but didn't inquire further. I didn't want to bring back unpleasant memories or upset the child who was listening to our conversation.

"Hi Oliver."

He didn't answer. I ran through the standard pre-anesthetic questionnaire with his mother—medications, allergies, recent illnesses, family history of anesthetic problems. Her family members had had no issues with anesthetics, but she wasn't sure of the family history on Oliver's father's side.

I scrutinized the child from the side of the crib. He looked a little sick. He had no intravenous.

"Did they have trouble starting an intravenous downstairs?" I asked.

"They said it looked hard and that they would leave it for you."

This was better than the emergency department nurses messing up the few suitable veins he might have by poking at them and missing. I listened to his chest with my stethoscope, but he began to cry, making it difficult to hear.

I backed off. I would ordinarily have told the mother to hold the child on her shoulder to comfort him and then listen. Picking him up would probably cause pain. "Parker, do you have any questions?"

"No." She looked very worried. A tear streamed down her cheek.

"No needles," Oliver screamed.

Children are affected by and amplify the anxieties of their parents before surgery. Single parents radiate more fear. Boy patients are worse than girls. Sara and I wheeled the crib with a crying and thrashing Oliver into the operating room. When Sara carried Oliver to the operating table, he clung to her like a cat with its claws out. I turned on a gas mixture to flow through the anesthetic tubing. He was fighting and screaming, refusing to let me apply the mask.

"Oliver, I've got a pilot's mask for you to wear," I said. "You could play that you're flying an airplane, like on TV."

"No mask! No mask!" the child screamed.

"Sara, can you please hold the mask for Oliver while I start an intravenous? Just lightly cup it on his face and follow him when he moves."

Sara took my seat at the head of the table. "We have two flavours of mask today, Ollie—chocolate—or *delicious,* yummy broccoli," she said. "I think you might like the broccoli."

"Chocolate! Chocolate!" the child screamed.

Nitrous oxide has no odour, and sevoflurane gas smells like gasoline. Sara innocently applied the mask, which the child readily accepted. "You have to really breathe it deeply four or five times before you taste the chocolate."

In a few seconds the child quietened. I started the intravenous, injected propofol to induce sleep and a paralyzing agent, and then changed places with Sara at the head of the table. While illuminating the child's throat with a laryngoscope, I passed a tube into the trachea. Sara pressed on the neck to prevent regurgitation of stomach contents. I may have brushed against Sara's chest when we changed places.

"You're really good with children, Sara," I said. "Don't you feel guilty about lying?"

"No. Everyone lies."

"Sorry. I may have accidentally brushed against your boob."

"Oh, I didn't notice." Sara's eyes were twinkling.

Chandler came into the room and Sara said, "Okay, we're ready. Scrub-a-dub-dub please."

The surgery was uneventful. If Chandler knew about Katya's cancelling her colonoscopy with him, he didn't let on or it didn't bother him. He conversed pleasantly with me about having a son almost Oliver's age as he worked.

When Chandler was done, Sara and I moved the patient back onto the crib. It had a bulky design to keep its occupant imprisoned. I pushed from the back so I could watch that Oliver didn't dive off as we walked. Sara steered, holding the side rail. The hallway was cluttered with cast equipment and a cart for X-ray gowns and Chandler standing by the scrub sink. Sara shifted to the front of the stretcher as we passed him.

He said, "You could have fit."

"It would have made you uncomfortable, Chandler." Sara's tone was flirtatious.

After we had settled Oliver in the recovery room, I went to the waiting area to update Parker. She was teary-eyed.

"Hi Parker. Everything went well. Oliver is just waking up in the recovery room. They will call you in to see him in a few minutes."

"Oh, thank you so much," she sobbed.

"If you live in town, he might be able to go home later today. The surgeon will talk to you."

"Okay."

"You said that Oliver's father was out of the picture. Did he pass on?" I was still wondering whether his father was Albert Yantzi.

"He's not dead. He moved away. I spoke to him a few weeks ago and he's not interested."

When divorced spouses say something like this, it might be true, but it's equally likely that they are punishing their former spouse by keeping them in the dark about their child's life.

"Okay, just wait here then for a few minutes until one of the nurses comes to get you."

At 7:45 a.m. the next morning, 15 minutes after I stopped being on call for anesthesia, I got a call from the coroners' answering service. A farmer had fallen to his death at a farm property a short drive from Coventry. The house was occupied by an older couple. The paramedics had come and gone and police were on scene.

A uniformed constable, whom I recognized as Hunter Schultz, approached me when I arrived. After agreeing that we didn't need to exchange business cards, he explained that the accident had happened some time during the night. The husband had apparently fallen to his death onto a concrete slab from a second-floor doorway that used to open onto a deck. His wife slept in a separate bedroom at the opposite end of the house and claimed not to have heard anything. She discovered him by the side of the house in the morning.

After Hunter had finished briefing me, he took me to interview the wife. Mrs. Nora Collins was sitting at a large wooden desk in a tidy home office going through some papers. From a distance, they looked like life insurance documents. There was a blue plastic recycle bin on the floor beside the desk containing a pile of neatly stacked pages she had discarded. She was between 60 and 70 years old, wearing a crisp blue and white floral printed house dress. Her salt-and-pepper colour hair was coiffed. She stood and formally offered to shake my hand.

The three of us went into her nicely appointed living room together and were seated. Mrs. Collins stated that she last saw her husband Sindler alive at 10 p.m. the previous evening. She said that they slept separately because of his snoring. He was accustomed to drinking five to six beers every evening. He got up several times through the night to urinate and sometimes urinated out the door into the yard because the bathroom was farther to walk. She occasionally heard him moving furniture around in the room and wondered whether he was sleep walking.

They had been in the process of replacing the wooden deck adjoining the door from which her husband had fallen. The construction company started the job a month previously but hadn't come back to finish it. In typical fashion, they probably accepted and started several jobs to get customers committed, so there would be work to last through slower times. I didn't know what to make of her providing two alternative explanations, drunken urination and sleepwalking, for her husband's fall.

Mrs. Collins showed us to her husband's bedroom on the second floor. It had spartan furnishings. The bedframe looked like it was homemade with sawn wooden four-by-four-inch bedposts. The floor was unvarnished planks. There were two empty beer cans on a night table. There was nothing like a suicide note. The area of the house that Mrs. Collins inhabited was much nicer.

The constable and I went outside to the back yard. Sindler's bedroom door was about ten feet above the concrete pad. There was a one-foot diameter dried circle of blood with a clear serum cap on the cement. Linear streaks of blood radiated out from the circle in a splash pattern. A trail of blood drops led to the side of the house. There were blood smears on the white siding.

Sindler was lying beside the house in the grass, clad in long underwear, socks and a jacket. There was a gash on his forehead and a right peri-orbital hematoma. The knuckles of both hands were abraded but no limbs were broken. He was cold and in full rigor mortis. That meant he had been dead for at least six hours.

The blood splatter showed an impact pattern where he had struck his head on the concrete below the door. He had gotten up and staggered to the side of the house, heading for the front door, leaving a trail of circular blood drops. He had wiped his head with his right hand and smeared blood from his hand along the siding before suffering a terminal collapse.

Branko approached us from the driveway. "Hi Matt. I was here earlier, but I had to leave to attend to another call. What do you make of it?"

"This is a first for me. It looks like he got up to pee, chose the doorway because it was closer than the bathroom and forgot the deck was gone. His wife says he was a sleep-walking drunk."

"Cause of death?"

"He'll have to go for an autopsy. It might be the head injury. I wouldn't be surprised if he also bled into his chest or pelvis. No long bones are broken so he absorbed the energy of the fall somewhere else. What is chilling is that I could see myself doing the same thing."

"In my youth, when I first moved to Canada, I used to pee in the sink in my flea-bag rooming house where the bathroom was down the hall," Branko said.

"I've done that too," Hunter said.

"Are you finished speaking with the wife?" Branko asked me.

"Yes. She seems nice, but not in a profound state of mourning."

"I interviewed her earlier. I don't think she did it," Branko said.

"Unless she was up in his room when he was peeing and gave him a push."

"Unlikely. The other way around, I would believe. His dick is still inside his long johns. You said he's going for an autopsy?"

I nodded.

"Hunter, can you call Christobel's? That's who the wife wants. Guess who we arrested a few days ago, Matt."

"The guy who killed the Sherman couple who owned the drug company in Toronto?"

"Close. We pinched Caleb Yantzi. We were keeping an eye on him when he got into a disagreement with a neighbour. They were both in horse-drawn Mennonite buggies. Noah claimed that Caleb threatened him with a shotgun. Caleb said that Noah threw a whiskey bottle at him. Noah said that Caleb's father Albert owed him money and now that Albert is gone, Caleb should do the right thing and assume the debt. Caleb said that Noah is a drug dealer who got his drugs from Mexico. Noah said Caleb stole his ladder."

"He said, he said. Who to believe? They both sound so convincing. What did you do?"

"Caleb's shotgun was loaded and unsecured, so we arrested Caleb and confiscated the weapon."

"Is Noah a drug dealer?"

"Maybe. He has no record."

"Is Caleb still in custody?"

"No. We let him go a few hours later, but we've got his fingerprints and palm prints on file now," Branko said optimistically. "Noah stated that Caleb stole his ladder, so just out of interest, we checked his palm print against the print on the Winchester that killed Albert, and it didn't match. There's no reason it should, of course. Why would he kill his own father?"

"What's the likely penalty for Caleb?"

"It's his first offence, so probably just a fine. Noah agreed that Caleb didn't actually point the gun at him."

Sindler Collins' autopsy was done the next day. It showed intracranial bleeding, bilateral rib fractures, multiple pelvic fractures, a lacerated bladder and extensive hemorrhage into the pelvic cavity. Both the head injury and the hemorrhage would have been sufficient to kill him. I called Mrs. Collins, expressed my condolences and told her the result. She took the information without emotion and politely thanked me for calling. Mr. Collins had two reasons to have fallen out of his elevated doorway and the autopsy showed two causes of death.

Chapter 15

My phone was ringing. I glanced at the time. It was 9:30 a.m., which meant the night had netted me six hours of sleep. The call display said Sean Feeney. I picked up without hesitation.

"Hi Matt. Are you doing anything today? Tyson and I are going golfing. Do you want to come?"

"With you and Tyson?"

"Yes. Come with us. I have a tee-time for 11 a.m. It'll be grand."

"Doesn't Tyson have to be in school?"

"Matthew, you can't learn survival skills in school. I've given him the day off."

"Golf is a survival skill?"

"It can be, yes, for networking. You won't have a social life after you retire without golf."

"Did you run it past your school principal?"

"Don't be ridiculous."

"I'd like to come. I have really no idea where the ball is going any time I swing."

"You just need a few lessons and some practice. You're a natural athlete."

"Okay. I need to shower and have a cup of coffee."

"Have a bite of breakfast too. I don't want you fainting. We're going to have a late lunch after we play. Pick you up in half an hour."

I staggered in and out of the shower and found Katya making the bed. She was only working half-time this semester.

"I thought you wanted to sleep late. Who was that on the phone?"

"Sean. He wants to play golf." Having just come from the bathroom, I free-associated to Katya's colon. "I saw Chandler at the hospital yesterday. He didn't seem too upset at your having cancelled your appointment. Maybe he doesn't know about it."

"I rescheduled the appointment with him for next week. My family doctor said it would be months and months before she could get anyone else and that he had a good reputation."

"I said I could get you someone else."

"No. It's fine. I hear he's very good-looking."

"Okay then. I'm happy if you are."

I had nearly choked down a muffin when the doorbell rang. Sean was standing on the porch.

"Top of the morning, boyo!"

I could see it was a beautiful day, sunny and cool. "Looks like a perfect day. Can I offer you some coffee." I held up my cup.

"No thanks, Matthew. I had mine hours ago. You can bring your coffee with you."

I glanced at my watch. "My stuff is in the garage. I'll come out through the garage door."

My golf bag had never been used. Katya had given me the clubs as a Christmas present following advice from Sean on what to buy. I stowed it in his trunk, carefully laying the bag on top of two other golf bags, so as to give the impression of not being rough with his clubs.

"Nice bag. You haven't even peeled the plastic off the clubs."

"No, not yet."

"You on call last night?" he asked.

"Yes. I actually slept six hours."

"You look all right. We're just going to pick up Tyson. He's never golfed before, so you don't have to worry about being hung over or out of practice."

"How often are you golfing now, Sean?"

"Three times a week anyway. I would like to give Tyson a taste of how his life could go. He's had some tough breaks and he is at a crossroads. He's with a pretty good family now."

"What's their motivation to take him in? Do they know about his criminal record?"

"They do it for the extra money. They know he's had some trouble. He has no record because he's underage."

"They must be nice people to take the risk."

We drove across town and into the driveway of a modest three-bedroom house in a thirty-year-old subdivision. Tyson was waiting in the driveway. He was wearing dark green cargo shorts and a cream-coloured polo shirt. His blonde hair was cut short and styled. Except for the cigarette, he could have been in a catalogue for back-to-school wear.

"Hello Mr. Feeney and Dr. Kork. Nice day isn't it." He grinned, seemingly at the propriety of it all.

"Hi Tyson," we echoed.

"I borrowed my son's clubs for you, Tyson," Sean said. "I told him you would take good care. They're in the back."

"How are your new living arrangements?" I asked.

"Good. It's a nice family. They have two other kids, so I'm not alone here."

"Are they your age?"

"No. They're only eight and ten. I'm like their older brother," he said grinning again.

We drove 20 minutes out of town to a club with rolling hills and lush green scenery.

"You golfed here before?" Sean asked.

"No. It looks lovely."

"It's cheaper because it's out of town. I joined here for the season. You know, my father owned a golf course that I had to maintain. That might give me an advantage."

"That, and playing three times a week."

Sean paid Tyson's greens fee and got a bucket of balls for the driving range. "We have some time for a warm-up."

We congregated around Sean for some instruction: "Keep your eye on the ball. Hold the club like a tube of toothpaste. Picture a partially deflated beach ball between your arms. Keep your eyes on the ball. Don't look up."

Tyson and I nodded sagely. Tyson topped the ball with his first swing. I hit the dirt. On my second try, I missed the ball entirely and came around 360 degrees for a second try.

"Relax Matthew," Sean said. "Keep your left arm straight. One-two, follow-through. Easy does it."

The majority of athletic games are a variation of stick and ball. Golf is stick hit ball and then go look for it. I'm not good at finesse games like billiards or golf. I want to do better by trying harder. I heard a satisfactory smack as my club face connected with the ball.

"Okay, let's go," Sean said.

By the fourth or fifth hole, I was connecting with every fifth or sixth shot. I noticed that Tyson was now connecting about every second shot. He had an easy smile when he hit a shot cleanly.

Sean's drives were landing not far from the greens. His second shot would be on, and then one or two putts would put the ball in the hole.

"It's a beautiful day anyway," I said.

"Look at how Tyson's manner is getting more confident," Sean said.

"I noticed. He has some natural ability."

I repeated all the mantras in my head about keeping my eye on the ball and my left arm straight and connected with my drive on the eighth hole. Tyson took a drag on his cigarette. "Good shot, Dr. Kork. You're going to be good at this sport if you picture a partially deflated beach ball between your arms."

"That's just what I was doing."

We stopped for lunch after nine holes. The clubhouse was populated by comfortably overweight, retired, middle-class men congregating with their friends over rounds of beer. These men were dedicating the rest of their lives to perfecting their golf swings and enjoying status with their peers when they played well. They were happy to have a purpose. They were exactly where they should be.

We studied the menus. "Golf is not a man's game," I said. "It doesn't require strength and stamina, just finesse." I noticed Sean wink at Tyson.

I was hungry and decided on a boar-burger, fries and a salad. We ordered a dozen wings to start.

"What music do you listen to, Tyson?" I asked while we waited for the food.

"I like the old stuff—Led Zeppelin, Doors, Nirvana. Your generation had better music than mine."

This could have been sycophancy, but my son told me the same thing.

"It was a really big deal to us too. Musicians were our heroes. I remember arguing with my friends over what album covers meant when I was your age."

"That's all gone with streaming," Sean said.

"Maybe they didn't mean anything," Tyson said.

I considered the insight. "Tell me about your home when you were growing up."

"My father's cell phone was always ringing. His sketchy friends were always dropping by most nights, smoking dope. My dad worked as a contractor doing home renos. He took me along to jobsites on weekends and on weekdays when he needed me. We were kind of partners for the last few months. He'd be up all night, then we'd go to work in the morning building a deck or renovating somebody's kitchen."

"What was his company called?"

"Best Construction."

I wondered whether Katya had ever called them for an estimate and if she knew Mr. Gruber was a drug dealer. "How was he able to work without sleep?"

"It wasn't every night," Tyson said. "I remember some pill parties. They had a mix of different coloured pills in an aluminum pie plate on the kitchen table like candies. Each guy would take a turn washing down a pill with a swig of whiskey until someone dropped… He never pushed any drugs on me. He took his responsibility as a dad fairly seriously. He even drove me to early morning hockey."

"What was life like when your mother was still with you?"

"I don't remember it too well. She loved me. She was a drug user. I found her lying in bed when I got home from school. There were empty pill bottles on the night stand. She put out pictures of me when she was holding me as a baby and another of me in shorts and a T-shirt when I was five. Our dog was up on the bed with her whining."

"How old were you?"

"Seven."

"That's rough. Where was your dad when it happened?"

"He was away on a job. I called the police and they got him to come back. The labels on the bottles were for escitalopram, oxycodone, sertraline and Percocet. I studied them for a long time."

"Did she leave you a note?"

"Yes. The note said, 'I love you Tyson. I'm sorry for leaving you. Thank you for sharing your life with me. We'll meet again in a better world.' "

Sean kicked me under the table. The wings arrived and we tucked in.

"Sorry for bringing up the past," I said.

"It doesn't bother me. I've told it lots of times."

"Thank you for telling me. My mum died when I was a kid too."

"My dad made me smuggle satchels full of golf-course cash across the American border to avoid taxes," Sean said. We were united by hard luck stories.

The rest of the food arrived. Tyson finished off two hamburgers. When his plate was clean, I noticed he was surreptitiously eyeing the remaining wings.

"Go for it," I said. "I'm stuffed."

"Me too, boyo." Sean pushed the wings over in front of Tyson.

"Well, I enjoyed this more than the golf," I said.

"Matthew, you should come out more if you want to improve. You need to develop muscle memory. I'll call you next week for a game."

"I'll come but I don't love the game enough to play regularly. Each increment in my ability from practice might be offset by an age-related decline."

"Hogwash! People like what they're good at. You need to lay the foundations for retirement and a social life. You won't be able to rely on work to fill up your time."

"To that point—golf is the most popular in English speaking countries. In countries where it isn't considered gay for men to get together over lunch or a cup of coffee, it doesn't have nearly the following. Hardly anyone plays in Greece or Italy."

"I'll play," Tyson said.

Sean dropped Tyson off first and then drove me home. He held the trunk lid open for me to retrieve my clubs and said, "That went pretty well, I think."

"Has his father been in touch with him again?"

"Tyson said he texted him from a number he didn't recognize. It must have been a burner phone because it was disconnected right after. His father said he had to lay low for a while longer, until things cooled down, that he wouldn't be able to be in touch."

"It sounds like he's in jail somewhere in a foreign country."

"I think that boy may be going to university. His marks have really improved. The admissions people only look at the marks from the last three years of high school. In fact, I'm already looking at ways he can apply for bursaries and scholarships."

"He's not who I thought he was," I admitted.

Chapter 16

The day for Katya's colonoscopy arrived. She seemed composed as we got in the car together, although she had been up pooping throughout the night because of laxatives she had to take in preparation. The clerks greeted me warmly and called us almost immediately to check in. The preferential treatment was nice. It was what I tried to provide for my comrades-in-arms.

We were shown to a cubicle to wait. I was glad I had taken the day off. Sitting with Katya seemed important, because I could feel how we were giving each other courage. Also, I wanted to show the staff where I worked what a devoted husband I was. Our nurse, Kristiaan, gave Katya a hospital gown to put on, underwear off, open at the back. I stepped outside the cubicle curtain while she changed. It seemed immodest to stay.

"So, tell me what kind of guy your husband is," Kristiaan said in girlish conspiracy as he took her vital signs. I hadn't realized how much behind the scenes emotional support nurses do. Miller, the anesthesiologist assigned to the endoscopy room, gave me a smile as he passed pushing a patient on a stretcher.

Katya had an 11:30 appointment time. By 11:25, Miller had finished interviewing us and was wheeling her away. Twenty minutes later he brought Katya back barely conscious but looking none the worse. I stayed with her until she was awake enough to recognize me.

"Would you like ginger ale, orange juice or apple juice to drink? We also have digestive and arrowroot cookies," Kristiaan said, in the manner of an airline host.

"Apple juice please," Katya said

"I'm going to run down to the cafeteria," I said. "Do you want anything?"

"I want to go home to have a cup of tea."

"I thought you would say foot-long sub. You haven't eaten for two days."

I went downstairs to the coffee shop. An older woman volunteer approached the counter when she saw me.

"I'll have an egg salad sandwich on whole-wheat toast," I said.

"Oh, okay, okay. Will that be toasted?"

"Yes please. Put it in the paper, not the plastic take-out container please."

"Okay, will, is that on brown or white bread?"

"Brown."

"What kind of sandwich did you say that was again?"

"Egg."

I waited while she made the sandwich in slow motion. Retiree volunteers provide free labour at the hospital. You get what you pay for.

Coming back down the corridor to the O.R., I met Chandler on his way to the cafeteria to buy lunch. He stopped to talk.

"Is it true you were looking at my wife's bum? I heard some people talking," I said.

"No!"

"Okay… I believe you. How did it go?"

"It went well. Katya has a two-centimetre, sessile polyp that needs to come off." Sessile meant it was flat against the bowel lining without a stalk. "I made arrangements for her to go to Toronto to have it done."

"Okay. Did it look malignant?"

"No. It looks pre-malignant. It's smooth and non-ulcerated. I took a biopsy."

Katya was more awake when I got back to her cubicle. "How is your sandwich?" she asked.

"Soggy. It's in a sealed plastic container. You want a bite?"

"No thanks."

We waited out the mandatory hour together surfing on our phones. When Kristiaan said we could go, Bruno the porter brought a wheel chair for Katya.

Katya said, "It's okay. I can walk."

Bruno engaged the brake levers to hold the chair in place. "I have to wheel you to the door so youse don't have grounds to sue if you fall on hospital property. Also, I wouldn't have a job if everyone said that."

I collected Katya's things and we all went together to the front entrance of the building. Katya jumped out of the chair and walked the rest of the way to our car in the parking lot. We called thanks to Bruno over our shoulders, and he smiled and waved.

When we got home, I asked Katya what she wanted to eat.

"Just some tea and toast with a little blueberry jam."

"I thought you would be ravenous! How about some scrambled eggs and fat-back bacon?"

"No thanks." She sipped her tea and nibbled her food. "Did they say my polyp was pre-cancerous?"

"Yes, but Chandler said there's no indication of cancer yet. You still have to wait for the microscopic examination. Your father had bowel cancer, but he got it when he was 80. It's not hereditary any more at that age. You're not at any higher risk."

"Isn't bowel cancer hereditary?"

"After age 70, it's supposed to be due to declining immunity."

"Okay."

"So, you're just average risk."

"Okay."

"It isn't really fair that you got this. You do everything right. You eat all that salad."

"I do like meat, but I don't eat much smoked or preserved food and I cut out alcohol completely!"

"Hopefully, it's just a one off."

"I'm volunteering at the theatre tonight."

In addition to a movie theatre complex, we had a community theatre in Coventry.

"Are you sure you're up to it? How long have you been doing that?"

"I feel fine. I thought, since I'm retiring in a couple of years, I'm going to need some more activities. I've only been to the training course so far."

"You're not supposed to drive for 24 hours."

"I'm getting a lift from Sinead. She's the one who got me involved."

"You do look okay… But what if I come tonight and ask you a lot of annoying questions."

"I only have to tell you how long the play runs and where the washrooms are."

"I could get you in trouble."

"Go ahead and try."

"Dear Madame or Sir: I must have asked her ten times how long the play runs and where the washroom was, but she totally ignored me. She just kept talking to this cute guy. I don't know how to say her name, but on her nametag, it started with Kat and ended in ya. I had been so looking forward to the play and it completely ruined the experience for me. As an underweight, male, binary, heterosexual person of pallid colour, I am truly disappointed."

"Bastard."

Chandler's secretary called late that afternoon. Katya's repeat colonoscopy in Toronto was to be in two months. We were referred to a Dr. Fletcher at University of Toronto Hospital. Googling him revealed that he had about 20 research papers to his credit, although sometimes just as a fifth or sixth author. Medical journals try to cap the allowed number of co-authors for papers at six. Doctors in teaching hospitals add each other as authors to pad their academic credentials.

Dr. Fletcher had four stars out of five on Rate Your MD dot com. The consensus opinion in the positive five-star reviews was that he saved my husband's or wife's life. In the less numerous negative reviews, it was that he killed my husband or wife and never returned phone calls.

Sinead came over in her car to pick up Katya for her theatre shift, leaving me alone in the house. Knowing that Katya wasn't well made me feel unwell too. The waiting would be unpleasant for me, knowing that Katya had a ticking time bomb inside. In Coventry, I could call in a favour and jump the queue for surgery. Having no contacts in Toronto, I was unable to expedite the date for Katya's booking.

I felt a further Pavlovian sinking in my stomach. My cell phone was playing *Stargaze*, the non-threatening audio I had recently chosen as a replacement ring tone. Any ring tone can become threatening if it is paired with having to rush out to deal with some catastrophe. The call display showed Joshua Smith, the orthopedic surgeon. Orthopods are the carpenters and machinists of medical practice.

"Hi Matt. Sorry to bother you. I need to do an open reduction of a forearm fracture. He's eaten, so we can do it tomorrow morning. I tried a closed reduction in emerge, but the fracture is too unstable. You're on call tomorrow, I believe, right?" Non-urgent cases had to be fasted for six hours before surgery.

"Yes. What's the patient like?"

"He's a drunk Mennonite. Otherwise, young and healthy."

"Does he have health insurance?"

"I don't know. Let me check… No."

"How did he break his arm?"

"Believe it or not in a Mennonite buggy accident. I think they were racing. One buggy was passing another and one of the Mennonites fell off. He smells of alcohol."

"Okay. Is 9 a.m. okay? What's his name? I'll look him up."

"His name is Caleb Y-A-N-T-Z-I. Date of birth 5 January 1991."

"No kidding. I think I know him. Could you read the address off to me?"

I checked the address against the address I had for Caleb and Anna in my files, and it matched.

When I went to the hospital the next morning, I saw Caleb lying on a stretcher in a patient bay in the waiting area. Two cops were hanging around in the hallway just outside. They were both in uniform, big and burly. I walked over to where they were standing.

"How come you guys are here?" I asked. "Is Caleb Yantzi under arrest?"

"No. We were instructed to keep an eye on him."

"Hi Dr. Kork," the second cop said. "We could charge him with impaired driving, He reeked of alcohol and there was a smashed whiskey bottle on the road beside his buggy. The horse was waiting patiently for him to get up so they could finish fleeing to Mexico."

The first cop said, "We were already keeping an eye on his house, so we followed him when he pulled out in his buggy and we were right there when it happened."

"How impaired was he?" I asked.

"He was too banged up to blow into a breathalyzer. We asked the emerge doc for a blood alcohol sample but he said he didn't need it and he wouldn't order it just for us. Looks like Caleb will get away with this one."

"I would have ordered it for you," I said.

I went over to where Caleb was lying on his stretcher. "Hi Caleb. Long time, no see."

"Hi," he said back.

I picked up his chart to review it. "How much did you have to drink last night?" I would have to give him smaller doses of anesthetic agents if he was already partially anesthetized.

"I got hit in the head by a whiskey bottle from a buggy."

I noticed that Caleb did indeed have a bruise on the left side of his forehead.

"So, you weren't drinking?"

"No. I didn't tell the cops so I don't get them in trouble. It was Noah Shetler prob'ly," Caleb said sullenly.

"Where were you going?"

"I was going to the horse auction. That's where we were all going."

"Were you racing?"

"Yes."

"Do you need a faster horse?"

"I like to go to see what newer models they got and to hear the auctioneer."

"With the number of times you're coming to the hospital, Caleb, you should apply for health insurance. It's free and you're paying for it anyway through your taxes." He probably didn't declare income or pay taxes.

"Send me a bill."

I pushed Caleb's stretcher through the doors of the operating room, got him hooked up to the monitors and started an intravenous. He meekly went to sleep at the command of propofol, the standard anesthetic induction agent. I passed an endotracheal tube into his windpipe and turned on the sevoflurane gas.

The circulating nurse Kristiaan put a tourniquet on Caleb's upper arm and prepped the skin with antiseptic. Josh made a long linear incision in Caleb's forearm to expose the bones. The scrub nurse

Nancy clanked various metal plates with screw holes together, arranging them on her table in order of length.

"Hey Matt, listen to this." Josh took a mallet from the nurse's table and tapped out a perfect rendition of "Mary had a little lamb" on the plates, xylophone style.

"That is fucking amazing." I sang along, off-key karaoke, "Whose fleece was white as snow, and everywhere that Mary went the lamb was sure to go." It really was amazing.

"If it rhymes, it must be true," Josh said.

"How did the accident happen?" Kristiaan asked.

"The way I heard it, he got drunked up and fell off his buggy on the way to a horse auction," Josh said.

"He says he was pushed by a flying whiskey bottle," I said.

"They can fly, Matt?" Kristiaan asked.

"From another buggy."

"You're joking!" It was Kristiaan's turn to be amazed.

"I suspect they fly better when they're empty."

Josh chose a five-hole metal plate from Nancy's table and lined it up to span the fracture site. "I have in fact been to one horse auction myself," he said. "It was entertaining. Good as TV. Mennonite families crowd around, seated on hay bales surrounding the perimeter of a courtyard, the cool kids with long grass stems between their teeth. Proud stallions are paraded in and out, and the rapid-fire auctioneers get people all riled up."

"Cool!" Kris said. "I like the sound of proud stallions."

"I read through the note you dictated for this guy, Josh," I said. "Do you mind if read back a few lines?" I pulled up his note on the monitor beside me, ready to go.

"Be my guest."

"This 31-year-old Man of Night stained a fall from the height five feet stained fracture four arms, door slang ulnar this placement of the mid-shaft ray deus murder accomplice shot a guy in the head for insurance money."

"Does it really say that?"

"Some of it."

"Well, that's the dictation system for you. The cheapest option is often not the best choice."

"I'm just saying, in case you want to fix it."

"Read the disclaimer at the bottom."

" '*Not responsible for inaccuracies transcribed by a substandard automated dictation system.*' It did manage to type that correctly."

"Yes. It's got incremental learning. It knows that line from hearing it so often."

"When Hal becomes sentient, he slash she slash it, parentheses, his slash hers slash its, close parentheses, will hunt you down and kill you."

"Bring it," Josh said, brandishing a battery-powered drill to screw a metal plate in place. "Building me an off-the-grid robot with a one-metre drill bit pecker and circular-saw arms."

Orthopods will be amongst the last bipeds standing after the Great War Against the Machines.

Chapter 17

Walking down the hallway to the operating rooms, I passed the O.R. clerk Penny and gave her a wave. She sat in a glass partitioned office with the entrance facing away from me. She wouldn't have heard a verbal greeting. She waved back vigorously with a piece of paper fluttering in her waving hand.

I detoured into her office and Penny handed me the slip of paper. "A guy from some insurance company wants to speak with you. He said to call him back at this number."

I glanced at the note which read, *Howard Mifflen, Pan-Provincial Life* and a ten-digit telephone number. "How long ago did he call?"

"About two minutes," she said.

It was 7:35 a.m. "He must get to the office early." I stuffed the note in my shirt pocket and carried on down the hallway to start my day. I was doing a list of D&C's and hysterectomies. Adam was the surgeon and a new, young family doctor named Mason was assisting.

Adam was waiting outside the room. "You'll like the patients today, mon. They are all young, healthy, no medications, not overweight."

"You know all the magic words to say, Adam. I thought one of the hysterectomies had cancer." I had looked up the patients at home the night before.

"Yes, but she's nice and thin." Everything about anesthesia and surgery was easier with thin patients.

With Sara's help, I got the first patient asleep. Adam and Mason entered the room holding their washed arms up in the air. The scrub nurse gowned them and Sara tied their gowns at the back. Adam and Mason took up their positions on opposite sides of the O.R. table.

Sara was watching Mason. "So, do you have any children?" she asked him conversationally.

"Yes. My daughter Emily just won the Kiwanis Music Festival."

"Good sperm, Mason!" I said.

"Thanks," he replied.

"So, do you do any obstetrics?" Sara asked Mason. "The old family doctors all did OB."

"No. I don't want to get up nights."

"Are you accepting new patients into your practice?"

"No. I'm already full."

Sara lost interest in Mason. "Any good coroner cases lately, Matt?" she asked.

"No. It wouldn't be breaking confidentiality to tell you that most calls have to do with old people dying at home. The police call me because there is no family doctor or they don't know how to contact the family doctor after hours."

"A lot of people can't get family doctors. My mother's doctor retired and she can't find a new one," Sara said. Twenty per cent of Canadians couldn't find family doctors anymore and were forced to clog up emergency rooms.

"I got an interesting call to a nursing home recently," I remembered. "An older woman with dementia was sitting in her wheelchair when another nursing home resident tripped and fell over her. She was sent to hospital where they discovered she had a fractured hip. After speaking with the relatives, the doctors decided not to operate because she was so demented. They sent her back to the nursing home where she was treated with hydromorphone and died."

"Why is an anesthesiologist going to nursing homes?" Adam asked, his voice getting shrill. "Why don't you just do more of my add-on cases so I don't have to wait until 11 o'clock at night for my turn to operate and then have my case cancelled because it's too late in the day? I'd like to do an add-on today incidentally," he added, his tone now half-heartedly conciliatory.

"I have to get out occasionally. The death was considered accidental, so I had to go see her. It turned out she was a university professor. The nurse at the home told me that the guy who tripped over her had a history of violence. He'd punched one of their nurses in the face. I went to see him on the ward and he was young to be in the home, only in his sixties. He was pacing constantly and wouldn't speak. It turned out he was the former vice-president of a big life insurance company. The question was whether this was an accident or a homicide. Did he trip over her intentionally?" I couldn't remember if the insurance company was Pan-Provincial.

"What about my add-on?" Adam asked.

"We'll have to see how the list goes," I answered.

"Insurance executives are aggressive," Adam said. "They have to work their way up from sales and answer to their shareholders, an' all o' dat shite."

"I had to call it an accident. He was demented too, but he wouldn't tell me how demented."

"Why are you here assisting instead of working in your office?" Sara asked Mason. "A high-school dropout could hold that retractor."

"I have to get out occasionally," Mason said.

The first case went uneventfully. The four of us got ready to slide the patient back onto her stretcher.

"Turn the patient on three. Three!" I said to lighten the mood. People groaned. "Okay then. One, two, buckle my shoe, three," and we turned her onto her side on the stretcher.

Adam had saved the patient with cancer for later in the day. A scraping of cells from the inside of her uterus during a D&C had shown cancer cells. She was having a hysterectomy and bilateral salpingo-oophorectomy—uterus, fallopian tubes and ovaries. She was probably very curable.

Her uterus was quite large. Adam assured me that this was due to benign uterine fibroids, not cancer. I didn't doubt Adam's capabilities, but when I saw the size of her uterus, I went to the phone to order a cross match of blood just in case.

"I am the slip of the knife. I am also it's recipient." Adam was offended, but that couldn't be helped.

"Why do you take the tubes and ovaries out if she has uterine cancer?" Mason asked.

"There might be secret cancer. It saves coming back for a recurrence. It might be safe to leave the ovaries. Generally, if you have carcinoma in situ, you get a small operation. If you have a recurrence, you get a big operation. If you're incurable, you don't get any operation. If you're hopeless, we're not going visit you anymore."

As the day wore on, the conversation tapered off.

"This newer generation of doctors is so different from the older one," Sara said to the room. "They are all into biking and lifestyle and family. None of them say the S-word or the B-word or the C-word."

"Only female surgeons can use the C-word," Adam said.

Mason said, "Hey Sara, call my office about your mother. Tell my secretary I told you to call." He could take a hint after all.

After we did Adam's add-on, I passed Penny in her office, getting ready to leave. "He called again," she said.

"Who?" I asked.

"Howard from Pan-Provincial. He says it concerns a patient of yours and that it's important."

I had totally forgotten about the slip of paper in my breast pocket and pulled it out to look at it again. "Thanks, Penny. I probably would have thrown the number in the wash with my O.R. greens."

It didn't seem like Howard was going to go away. I was tired and didn't feel like calling him. After driving home, I picked up the phone anyway.

"Hi. This is Dr. Matthew Kork in Coventry. You wanted to speak with me."

"Yes. Thank you for calling back, Dr. Kork."

"How can I help you?"

"My name is Howard Mifflen. I'm in charge of the claims department at Pan-Provincial Life in Toronto. We're looking into a claim for death benefits for a Mr. Albert Yantzi. You were the coroner in that case, I believe."

"Yes, that's correct."

"Do you remember the case or would you like a few minutes to review your files? The beneficiary, a Ms. Taylor McGuire, has signed a release allowing you to speak candidly with us about this matter."

"I remember the case," I said. It was nice that Taylor had given him my work and not my cell number. I decided to carry on the conversation as a favour to her.

"We would be happy to compensate you for the time you take in assisting us, Dr. Kork."

"That's okay. I don't imagine this will take too long." I didn't want to be financially beholden to him or feel motivated to assist him in denying Taylor's claim.

"We also tried contacting a second beneficiary, the decedent's son, a Mr. Caleb Yantzi. He seems to barely speak English. He told us that Taylor could speak for the both of them."

Caleb must have recognized that Taylor was smarter and better looking than him. "Caleb is a traditional Mennonite. His first language is low German, but he can speak English when he chooses. He's not much of a talker," I said.

"Yes, well, there are several red flags here, I'm afraid. If you can help us sort out some questions we have, it might improve Ms. McGuire's chances of having her claim accepted."

"There are limits to what I can tell you, but go ahead and ask."

"Although Mr. Yantzi died with a life insurance policy in place, the policy was less than three months old. That is more than a little suspicious. There are very few coincidences in my line of work. If Mr. Yantzi suicided within two years of the date that the policy was underwritten, it is automatically voided."

"Yes. I've heard that was the case with life insurance."

"You have submitted a finding of *undetermined* as the manner of death on the claim application that Ms. McGuire forwarded to us. What did you mean by that?"

"It means that there wasn't enough evidence to make a decision."

"The standard for you, I believe, is the balance of probabilities. Mr. Yantzi died of a gunshot wound to the head. That certainly rules out a death from natural causes. It suggests suicide, accident or homicide. Can you tell me, on the balance of probabilities, which way you would lean?"

"They seem equally probable," I said.

"Is it likely that more evidence will be forthcoming?"

"It's possible, but we are three months out now. Out of interest, do life insurance companies pay death benefits when the manner of death is undetermined?"

"Certainly, we do, in certain circumstances, unless *undetermined* is a placeholder and more evidence is likely to be forthcoming. Is that likely to be the case here?"

"I don't know. It seems unlikely."

"In your investigation, Dr. Kork, did you uncover any evidence that Mr. Yantzi was depressed, took antidepressant medications or had suicidal ideation?"

"Do you have access to his medical files?"

"Yes. Mr. Yantzi signed a blanket release for electronic medical records, prescription drug records, driving records, police reports, criminal records, tax returns and psychological therapy records with his policy application."

"Then you know that he had an expired prescription for antidepressants, like fifteen per cent of the general population."

"Had he ever seen a psychiatrist?"

"Not to my knowledge." I decided not to mention Albert's diary musings. They were open to interpretation. He didn't specifically threaten suicide. Taylor could reveal the diary contents if she liked.

"Did you see any evidence that Mr. Yantzi had issues with drug addiction?"

Taylor had initially said that he didn't and then subsequently corrected herself. Her information was ten years old. "There were no drugs at the scene. There was nothing in Albert's electronic medical record to show that he used illicit drugs. I don't believe he had any arrests. Taylor told me her father had used drugs ten years ago. You can ask her the details." I didn't want to prejudice her case.

"Did you do a toxicologic analysis of Mr. Yantzi's blood or tissues."

"Yes, we did."

"What did that reveal?"

"That information is in the final coroner's report. I am not allowed to disclose the contents to you. Only the next of kin has access to that."

"Taylor McGuire has signed a release, allowing us to access the full coroner's report including toxicology."

"She will have to obtain it and forward a copy to you. I gave her instructions on how to get it by writing to the Office of the Chief Coroner. All documents are released centrally from that office."

"If Mr. Yantzi died while under the influence of any illegal substance, that would be grounds to deny Ms. McGuire's claim. Can you tell me whether this was the case?" Howard was sounding aggressive.

"I'm not allowed to. You should contact the Regional Supervising Coroner's Office. They might agree to release the coroner's report directly to you with Taylor's permission."

"Are the autopsy and toxicology reports included with the coroner's report?"

"Yes."

"Dr. Kork, we've decided to delay and contest the claim. The beneficiary, Taylor McGuire, will have to wait until our investigations are complete. You said that there is a one third chance of suicide. Suicide will invalidate the claim and the short interval is extremely suspicious. Life insurance policies are not intended to put beneficiaries in a better position than they would have been if the policyholder had survived. High risk behaviour, such as drug abuse, will also invalidate the claim."

According to all accounts, Albert had abused drugs. He must have lied on his insurance application. I said, "That's your prerogative, I guess."

"Furthermore, if we find that Mr. Yantzi made any material misrepresentation of the facts in his policy application or if he was engaging in any criminal activity at the time of his death, Ms. McGuire's claim will be refused. However, if you speak with Ms. McGuire, please remind her that if she has any hope of collecting, she must continue to pay premiums on the policy while we are pursuing our investigations."

Of course, they would like to continue to receive premiums. "I don't foresee myself speaking with her," I said.

Albert's electronic medical record didn't give evidence of his prior drug abuse. Neither did police records. Nevertheless, Taylor's claim would undoubtedly be denied. They didn't have to show that Albert had suicided. The toxicology showed hydromorphone and flubromazolam. While hydromorphone was available in Canada by prescription, flubromazolam was a designer benzodiazepine, not legally available anywhere in North America.

The insurance adjuster would have known that I couldn't disclose any of the information he requested directly to him. He was hoping for me to unintentionally leak the information or at least to give him a clue as to where to direct his investigation by my tone of voice. I gave him the contact information for Richard Tull's office so he could try his luck there.

Taylor should get a lawyer. Claim denials can leave room for interpretation. Maybe a lawyer could negotiate a settlement with a reduced payout. I intended to tell her that if our paths crossed again.

Chapter 18

The date for Katya's repeat colonoscopy in Toronto approached. We reserved a hotel room and drove to Toronto the night before. I didn't want to have a nervous breakdown fighting traffic on the day of her procedure. If Katya was anxious, she didn't show it. I was certainly anxious but I didn't tell her. Being aware of all the things that could go wrong amplified the feeling.

The downtown Sheraton was only a few blocks from University General Hospital. We parked underground and checked in at reception. I waved the hungry bellhops away and we wheeled our own luggage to the elevator. Katya began arranging her belongings on the dresser when we got to the room and I rushed to empty my bladder. Katya likes to unpack in hotel rooms, while I prefer living out of a suitcase for maximum mobility.

My cell phone rang. The call display showed a Coventry area number. I picked up because I was immune from having to respond to any sort of anesthesia or coroner duty.

"Hello. Sorry to bother you. This is Mrs. Nora Collins. Am I speaking with Dr. Kork?"

"Yes. Hi."

"In order for me to receive the benefits from my husband's two life insurance policies, the companies require some forms to be completed. I can fill in my part, but they specify that a physician with knowledge of the circumstances of my husband's death has to complete the cause of death sections. Other than you, there was no other doctor involved. Could I impose upon you to fill out the relevant sections in these papers? I would be willing to pay you for your time of course."

She was right that there wasn't anyone else. "I can do that," I said. "There is a fee of about $75 if I do the insurance forms for you, depending on how long they take." Sindler Collins' cause and manner of death were clear—multiple trauma secondary to descent from height, and accident. Sindler was a drunk. His death was tragic, but she might be better off without him.

"Thank you so much."

"You're welcome. Out of interest, what was the name of the construction company you had to do your deck?" I wondered whether they might face some liability for not coming back to finish the job in a timely fashion.

"Best Construction."

That was Zeke Gruber's company. The life insurance companies might try to sue him to recoup their loss.

"I'll give you an address where you can mail the forms," I said.

"Can I drop them off to you?"

"No, I'm sorry, Mrs. Collins. I don't have an office. My regular place of work is an operating room, and I'm currently pre-occupied with matters out of town."

I gave her my mailing address and rang off.

"Katya, have you heard of Best Construction?" I asked.

"No. Never heard of them."

"Well, don't get them. It's Tyson Gruber's father's construction company. Mr. Gruber goes to work sleep deprived, drunk and high."

"How much life insurance do you have, hon?" Katya had been listening in on my telephone conversation.

"None, hon."

"Why's that, hon?"

"I had ten-year term insurance when I first started working, but it's expired."

"What do I do if you die, hon?"

"Inherit."

Inheritance is free of profit margins and claim contestations. My thoughts turned to my stomach. Katya wasn't allowed to eat before her colonoscopy but I needed something.

I said, "I'm hungry. Maybe I should go down to the hotel restaurant by myself. I don't want to torture you by eating in front of you."

"No. I want to come. I like to see you enjoy yourself."

"It won't be that enjoyable if I know you're watching and can't join me."

"I don't want to be alone."

The restaurant was empty and we got a table by the window. The waiter who brought my meal was hovering. "How are the first few bites tasting?" he asked too soon after dropping my plate.

"Leave us alone please," I answered.

The bed was comfortable, but I heard Katya moving around a lot overnight. Her procedure was scheduled for 1 p.m. We were supposed to arrive at registration at 11:30 a.m., so we had a couple of extra hours in the morning to get ready. We were close enough to walk to the hospital. After checking out, we went down to the parking garage to lock our bags in the car and then up the ramp to the street.

"Blue pants brown shoes, blue pants brown shoes, blue pants brown shoes," I said, as three businessmen passed us on the sidewalk. "They all have the same uniform."

"Skinny pants and long pointy shoes. I think it looks good," Katya said.

"Blue pants brown shoes, false advertising" I said, as a hipster wannabe passed. "That last guy's got the uniform and extra-long brown shoes, but he's way too short and pudgy."

"He could attract a nice short girl," Katya said.

After getting lost a few times in the massive rabbit warren of hallways and building additions at the hospital, we eventually found the colonoscopy waiting area and took a number. Thirty minutes later, a nurse showed Katya where to change into a hospital gown, open at the back.

A stocky surgical resident, dressed in dank, operating-room greens, came over. Residents have finished medical school and are training in a specialty. He was bleary-eyed and greasy, with a gold chain separating black matted chest hair in the V of his top from the unshaven stubble on his neck. He briefly explained the procedure and held out a clip board with a consent form for Katya to sign.

"When do we meet Dr. Skinner?" I asked. We had never actually met or spoken with him.

"He's not here yet. I can ask him to come out to speak with you when he arrives."

"I don't want to offend you, but I would like the staff man, that is Dr. Skinner, to personally do the procedure," I said.

He looked disappointed but said okay.

After another hour of waiting together, an orderly came and wheeled Katya away. A nurse directed me back to the waiting room.

Colonoscopies should take about 20 minutes. When the time stretched to two hours, my anxieties began to mount. When there was no communication from the surgeon or nurses for three hours, I approached the receptionist to find out what was going on.

She said, "It's just taking a little longer. The surgeon will come out and talk with you."

"Okay, I'm just going to the coffee shop to buy a sandwich," I said. "I'll be gone about 20 minutes."

"Okay" she said cheerfully.

When I got back, the waiting room was mostly empty. I approached the receptionist again. "It's just taking a little longer than usual," she said. "The surgeon will come out and talk with you." I sat down and ate my egg salad sandwich without any appetite.

After another half hour, a tall, dark-haired, tanned and fit-looking man in greens came out and introduced himself as Dr. Skinner. "The polyp was very tightly adherent to the colonic wall," he said. "I injected saline submucosally to raise the polyp. I felt I could tease it off. Unfortunately, the colon was perforated. The risk was always there. It was recognized almost immediately. I sent the resident out to brief you, but you must have just left." This was delivered in a matter-of-fact tone with no suggestion of apology.

"How is Katya. Where is she?"

"She's fine. She's in the recovery room. We took her to the O.R. and closed the perforation. We sent someone out to brief you."

"I've been here almost continuously. No one came out."

"When we couldn't find you, I signed an emergency consent because Katya was too drowsy. We'll admit her for a couple of days just to be safe. You're an anesthesiologist, aren't you?"

"Yes. Does she have a colostomy?"

"Yes. It's the safest thing. There was likely some intra-peritoneal contamination. She can come back in six months for a reversal."

"Was the resident there during the procedure?"

"Yes."

"Did you personally do the procedure or the resident?"

"The resident was doing the procedure under supervision."

"I specifically requested that no resident be allowed to do the procedure."

"Yes, he told me. I must have forgotten about that. Teaching hospitals cannot function without residents. They have to be allowed to do procedures for their training to have any meaningful benefit. They are expected to stay up nights to take call, do all the ward work in looking after patients postoperatively, all the unglamorous jobs. They have to be rewarded by being allowed to do procedures."

He was justifying his oversight with high-minded ideas about the resident-slaves who did all his work for him.

"You might have honoured my request as a professional courtesy. Was your resident on call last night?"

"I'm not sure. He might have been. The risk of perforation might be as high as one in a hundred for the type of polyp your wife had. It's dealt with now. We've got her on some broad-spectrum antibiotics. It will take a few days for things to settle down."

"Were you in the room when it happened?"

"Of course."

I didn't want to piss him off because I still needed him to look after Katya postoperatively. I picked my next question to be less inflammatory. "I suppose she will need annual surveillance with colonoscopies now."

"Yes. For the next few years."

When I went to see her on the surgical ward, Katya smiled wanly and held out her hand for me. I grasped it and sat down beside her. She didn't say anything. I stood up and kissed her forehead. I was afraid of losing her. I couldn't imagine my life without her.

She had raging fevers for five days. She ended up in the intensive care unit, intubated and on vasopressors for septic shock. Holding her hand and kissing her cheek or her forehead became a routine occurrence. I commuted back and forth to Coventry twice and then decided to get an Airbnb apartment in downtown Toronto.

Val Papadopolis called me at home in Coventry. I was surfing through the options on the Airbnb website.

"Oh, hey Matt. Sorry to hear about Katya being in hospital."

"Thanks Val"

"Which hospital is she in?"

"University General."

"Yeah, that's what I heard. Do you remember that condo in downtown Toronto I was telling you about. Well, the owners have decided to temporarily take it off the market. The market has gone soft with all these rising interest rates. I could get you a sweet deal on a short-term rental. It's walking distance to the hospital."

"I was just looking at Airbnb properties downtown. I wouldn't need it for more than a week or two."

"The owners were thinking of listing it there, but they're picky about who they rent to. It's free right now."

"Free sounds good."

"I meant unoccupied. The price won't be any more than an Airbnb. Their thinking is that if you try it and you like it, maybe you'll end up buying. They prefer to rent to qualified buyers."

"I don't want to give you false hope, but I do need a place to stay. Can you email me the details. I'll be able to make a decision pretty quickly. Is it furnished?"

"There's some Ikea-quality stuff in there they used for staging."

"Thanks Val. This could work."

"Give my best to Katya."

I finalized the details and moved into the condo late that evening. It was a one-bedroom apartment in a high rise. It wasn't opulent and there was no doorman. The location was what recommended it.

When I visited Katya in the morning, she was awake but still unable to speak because of the endotracheal tube in her windpipe. She communicated a short message by writing on a page on a clipboard, which I held for her. The message was, "How are you and Michael and Madame Fifi?"

I said, "They are all great. Michael was here to see you while you were asleep."

She wrote back, "I love you and Michael."

"She looks ready to be extubated," I told her nurse. "When are the doctors making rounds today?" My manner might have been slightly menacing.

"Oh yes. She's much better. They should be around soon," she replied.

Katya was extubated and awake in the ICU when I went back to see her in the afternoon. Being able to hear her voice was almost overwhelming.

Dolly called that evening. After visiting Katya, my evenings were free, so I was almost happy to take her call.

"Hi Matt. Am I disturbing you?' she said.

"No. How are you, Dolly?"

"Pretty good for an old lady. It was my birthday today."

"Congratulations. If you don't mind a personal question, how old did you become?"

"Oh, just 72-years-young. I still feel like I'm about 60 in my mind."

"I'll send you a happy belated birthday card. Did you have a party?"

"No. There's no one left to celebrate with now Francis has passed on. Happy birthday to you as well! Your birthday is in two days, isn't it?"

"How did you know that, Dolly?"

"I keep a record of peoples' birthdays who are important to me. I remember seeing your parents celebrate your birthday as a kid. All the kids in the neighbourhood came. I remember even Wayney was there."

"Yeah. There were a lot of kids in the neighbourhood then."

"Do you think Wayney's biker friends hold a grudge against you, Matt?"

"I think Wayney was a lone wolf. He wasn't in a biker gang."

"Well, I don't know about that—the way he was dressed that day he ran into you."

"I'm not too worried. Gay men are into leather outfits too."

"Gay bikers can hurt you just as easy as straight ones."

"Okay Dolly. What else is new?"

"I was down to the drugstore to get my blood pressure pills refilled today and I was looking at all the vitamins they have there. Which ones would you recommend?"

"None of them if you're eating a balanced diet."

"I'm taking the vitamin B and the vitamin D. I saw that those ones are good in the newspaper. What do you think about the melatonin to help me sleep."

"It might help a little. Daily exercise and not napping during the day is the best approach."

"Okay Matt. Whatever you say. When do you think you'll be coming this way to see the old neighbourhood again?"

"I'm actually in Toronto now. Katya's in hospital here."

"Oh no! What's she got?"

"She's in University General Hospital in the intensive care unit with a hole in her bowel."

"Well, isn't that awful. I hope she's gonna be all right."

"Me too, Dolly. I've been quite worried. When I saw her today, she was starting to improve a bit."

"Matt, come over and I'll make you some soup. In fact, come stay here while Katya is in hospital. You need a proper home and someone to talk to while all this is going on. You'll see how much you like it when you get here." Dolly wanted to mother me.

"Thanks Dolly, but I prefer to be closer to her. I'm at a short-term rental downtown." The traffic between downtown Toronto and Scarborough is horrendous, so I didn't want to make the trip.

"Where is it? Would it be okay if I come and see you and visit Katya too?"

"That's very kind of you, but it would be an ordeal taking a bus and two subways. I could just tell Katya that you extend your best wishes." Since I wasn't willing to take two subways and a bus to her house, it didn't seem fair to ask a person that old to navigate the trip for little old me. She didn't know Katya at all. She might have seen her through her window when we visited when my father was still alive.

"Nonsense! What else have I got to do? Now, where are you staying?"

"I'm close to Bay and Gerard, but we could just meet at the hospital if you're sure you want to come all this way. The hospital would be easier to find."

"I've got my pen ready. Now read off your address."

I didn't know how difficult it would be for her to walk from the subway to the condo to the hospital. "I'm at 45 Hopkins Street, but let's meet at the hospital. The coffee shop is just inside the front entrance."

Chapter 19

I woke up in the morning with no idea where I was. I got up off the box spring and looked around. It was a very basic looking motel room. I peeked out the window. It looked like I was near the corner of Kingston and Midland Roads, in Scarborough. I was on the second floor. This was a few kilometres from where I had grown up. I was fully clothed but seemed to have no luggage.

My prescription glasses were missing from the night table where I would normally have placed them. There was an old-timey room key on the corner of a dresser by the door. I peed and glanced in the bathroom mirror. There was a bruise below my right eye. Over the years, I had had a couple of knocks on the head—from car accidents, doctors' recreational hockey, and now one more. I went down to the end of the hall and stumbled down a flight of stairs where I saw a lobby and a desk clerk.

"Hey. How are you?" I asked.

"Good. What can I do you for?"

"Ah..." I squinted at the numbers printed on my room key fob. "I'm in 206. Do you happen to know when I checked in?"

"You came late last night. You arrived here on foot."

"I have no recollection of that." I felt my tender right cheek. I drank a bit, but never to the point of blackouts or amnesia. Maybe I was in some type of accident. "Were you on then?"

"No another guy, but he told me. We only had three people staying."

"Did I have any luggage?"

"Do you have any now?"

"No"

"Then, no."

I felt in my pockets. I had my cell phone, but my wallet was gone. I could have called Katya, but I couldn't see to dial the number.

"Tell me again how I got here."

The desk clerk turned and opened a door behind him. He called into the room. "Hey Bill. Come and talk to the customer from 206 before you leave. You checked him in last night."

Bill appeared in the doorway. He was an older East Indian looking gentleman—narrow face, slight build—a complete stranger to me. "Hi Bill. Do you remember me? Did you check me in?"

"For sure I do. You said that I was looking wery tired. You who could barely stand up on your own."

"What? Did you happen to notice whether I had any luggage?"

"Your mother said that she would take it home with her. She said that it would give you a reason to wisit with her."

"My mother doesn't live on this planet." I wondered what I should do next. "Is the room paid for?"

"Your wery nice mother said that you could use your credit card to pay."

I shoved my hands into my front pockets again and patted my pants in behind. Just as Bill had predicted, I found a VISA card. Thank God mother was feeling generous. I handed the card to the first clerk. "Do you think you could call a cab for me please?"

"Where you wanna go?"

The only person I knew in the area was Dolly, who lived across the street from me growing up.

"Falmouth Avenue. It's near the corner of Brimley and Eglinton."

"But that is just where I live," Bill said. "Whom do you know there? There are just houses in that area."

"I was thinking of visiting mother, but I forgot her telephone number."

"You are a wery funny fellow. Since you are having those bruises, maybe you should go to the hospital instead to see what is making you so funny."

"Don't worry about me. I'm a doctor." I felt my sore cheekbone.

"You are a doctor for the eyes?"

Did he want a free ophthalmology consultation? "No, not that kind."

"You are looking squinty. Why don't you come in my car? I will take you."

Bill was leaving and I had no reason to return to the room. We set off in Bill's car.

"May I say so sir, it is wery nice of you to visit your mother. I visit my mother every year in India."

"Thanks. It's much farther for you."

"Oh yes. Every year. May I ask you sir, why you don't stay with your mother when you wisit her?"

"Is Bill the name your mother gave you?"

"My name is Bhavyesh Wickramasinghe. Bill is my nick-name, sir."

"Which do you prefer?"

"My name is Bhavyesh."

"Bhavyesh, it's because the house smells of urine."

"No sir. You must not be smelling that. You must love your mother however she is."

"I try, but it's hard."

"There is no try. There is only succeed."

Bhavyesh drove past my old house and let me off in front of Dolly's one-story, yellow brick bungalow. It had been a ten-minute trip.

"Thank you, Bhavyesh. She's my godmother, not my real mother."

I banged on the door and I saw that Bhavyesh was waiting by the curb. When Dolly opened, he drove off. Dolly was a thin, older woman with grey frizzy hair who bore a strong resemblance to Margaret Atwood. She was wearing a plain house dress with a polka-dot pattern. She leaned out toward me and whispered, "Hello Matthew."

"Hello Dolly. Did you take me to that no-tell motel on Kingston Road?"

She looked at me with concern. "You don't look too good. Come in."

I went in and Dolly closed and locked the door behind me. We went into the living room and she pulled the drapes shut. "I wished for you to visit me and you did," she said coyly.

"I remember telling you my address and you making a surprise visit. I remember having tea with you and you trying to talk me into staying with you."

"Well, why would you want to live all by yourself downtown? All you see when you go out is psychos and derelicts. You could have a real home here."

"Where are my luggage and my car?"

"I got your bag here. Did someone steal your car? Maybe Wayney's friends." She looked worried.

"How did I get here, Dolly?"

"The old neighbourhood has changed so much, Matt. You would hardly recognize it."

"You didn't answer my question. Do you know?"

"Francis and I never had children. Nobody visits me anymore. I want you to stay here while your wife is in hospital. You could visit her and this could be your home."

"What happened after you made me the tea?"

"Don't get mad. I made you some tea in the kitchenette and dissolved a few of my Xanax in the boiling water." Xanax or temazepam was a benzodiazepine sleeping pill.

She continued: "When you were sleepy, I went outside and got a cruising cab to stop. I grabbed your suitcase and the cabbie helped you out of the building. The cabbie said he was just finishing for the night and there was a discount for cash if the trip was off the meter. He must have seen my money when I opened my purse to count it."

"How much did you lose?"

"A few hundred bucks. I don't like the credit cards too much because you can't keep track of what you're spending."

My head was starting to hurt. "Can I use your bathroom?"

"Sure. Down the hall."

I walked down the corridor past the room I had slept in for one night years ago after my car accident. Pausing outside Dolly's bedroom, I peeked over my shoulder and went in. My suitcase was there under the bed. I pulled it out and routed around for my spare eyeglasses. Facing the bathroom mirror, I examined my evolving black eye. My nose wasn't dripping cerebrospinal fluid, so that was a positive.

I had had a few concussions and was prone to headaches and bouts of fatigue. They didn't affect my lifestyle, but it could be why Dolly's pills had such an exaggerated effect on me. I relieved myself and went back to the living room. Dolly was sitting where I had left her, fidgeting with a cigarette pack.

"So, Dolly, I found my suitcase."

"I got it under the bed of my room for you."

"Okay. So, then what happened?"

"The cabbie dumped it on the ground beside you."

"What?"

"When we were getting close, the cabbie slowed down and parked in a dark spot. He grabbed my purse and took all my cash. It happened real quick like he'd done it before. He told me to get out or else. Well, I got out and you were nearly unconscious, so he pulled you out, grabbed your wallet and took your cash too. You banged your head on the door on the way out. I panicked because I thought you might be angry. We were across the street from a motel so I checked you in and walked home."

"That's about three kilometers."

"You wouldn't have made it."

"Did you call the cops? Do you remember the name of the cab company?"

"No. I got my purse back. He dumped it on the street. I didn't have nothing important in it anyways. I didn't want to tell them about drugging you."

"You could have skipped that part."

"Here's your wallet with your ID. He just dropped it too. He didn't want your credit cards. I didn't leave it in the motel in case you would think I stole all your cash. How much did you lose?"

"About a hundred bucks. I'll call the cops."

"No. I don't want them to know the story. I don't remember the cab company or what the guy looked like. He was wearing a Covid mask."

"You don't remember anything else about him?"

"He had an accent. He could have been Iranian, or Mexican maybe."

"Any part of his licence number?"

"It was dark and he had his lights off when he drove away."

"Where are the glasses I was wearing, Dolly?"

"They got broken when the cabbie pulled you out of the car. You want the pieces?"

"All right." They might lend credence to her story.

"Okay. I'll get them. They're in the kitchen drawer."

I called after her, "I'm going to make a report to the police anyway, Dolly"

"Well, don't use my name."

"The story wouldn't make much sense without you in it."

I spent another hour with Dolly and then rolled my suitcase out the front door. Dolly looked disappointed but didn't try to convince me to leave it.

Her parting words were, "Happy birthday, Matt."

I said, "Thanks Dolly," as my suitcase bumped over the weather stripping at the bottom of her doorway.

I took public transit back downtown to see Katya. The longer I live, the more I realize how much it sucks to get old. I actually considered staying, but it was too far to commute and there would have been too much emotional baggage being across the street from my old house.

Although I don't think they would have charged Dolly with anything, I never filed the police report. She's sort of family and they might have given her a hard time about drugging me with her sleeping pills and kidnapping me.

Chapter 20

Residents came around once daily to do rounds on Katya and the other patients. The resident who had operated on Katya came by every third day, trying to avoid looking at me. I didn't ask him if he had been up all night on the day before he perforated Katya's colon. I was too angry to speak with him. I already knew that he had because I had asked one of his colleagues. I also know he didn't come to speak with me in the waiting room that day, probably because he was too afraid to face me.

One morning, I noticed a curly-haired man in his thirties walking toward me in the hospital lobby, casting me a friendly glance.

"Remember me?" he said as I passed.

He looked familiar but I couldn't remember why, so I stopped and waited.

"You gave me my anesthetic in Coventry. I had bowel cancer."

I remembered now. He had had a laparoscopy, a procedure where a probe with a video camera at the tip is inserted through the abdominal wall.

"Oh, yes. Hi! How are you doing?"

"They're sending me for chemo. I'm a fighter. I'm going to beat this," he said confidently and waited for my reaction. I gave him two thumbs up.

The cancer had been a complete surprise. He had peritoneal seeding. It was a peak and shriek, meaning just a very short procedure and a referral to a teaching hospital for chemo and radiation therapy. He would be dead in a few months. Hospitals are nests of terrible tragedy, low-risk obstetrics and total joint replacements being notable exceptions.

I could leave Madame Fifi in Coventry while I was commuting back and forth. Having moved into the condo, I had to figure out something else. Although Michael wasn't allowed pets in his apartment and I wasn't allowed pets in the condo, he was able to temporarily take her. His legal opinion was that the Landlord and Tenant Act precluded landlords from restricting pets once the tenants were ensconced.

Having too much free time, I bought some brown pointy shoes in one of the shops in the Eaton Centre. On the day before Katya was to be discharged from hospital, I drove over to Michael's apartment to get Madame Fifi. I brought her to the condo to help celebrate Katya's deliverance and because the dog stress-barked at night keeping Michael and his girlfriend awake.

The next morning, I put on some skinny blue jeans and the shoes, and drove my car into the hospital parking garage. I left the dog in the condo to wait. I was pretty sure that like our hospital, University General would have rules against yappy canines.

Katya's eyes widened as she looked me over. "You look good," she said. "I would do you."

"Thanks, hon." I picked up her overnight bag with her toiletries and underwear. "I would do you back."

There was a collection of flowers on the window ledge of Katya's room. I looked through the cards. They were mostly from friends and work colleagues in Coventry. There was one from the operating room that even a few of the surgeons had signed and one from Val Papadopolis.

One of the porters came to put Katya in a wheelchair. I waved him away and helped her into the chair myself.

"What would you like to do with all these flowers?" he asked.

"Can we just put the bouquets on the window ledges in the hospital lobby?" Katya asked.

"Sure. That's what a lot of people do."

Katya grabbed one of the bouquets. "I just want this one."

The porter pushed Katya's wheelchair to the front entrance of the hospital as I walked alongside with her bag. Katya was holding the bouquet that Michael had brought. The porter kept Katya company while I got my car and swung it into the circular driveway at the front of the building. I thanked him for waiting.

"It's better than pushing wheelchairs. It's nice to get a breath of air."

"I hear you. Hospital air used to make me gag," I said.

"I was an English teacher in Japan for two years. There wasn't much work when I got back." He wasn't an ordinary porter. People tell you what's top of mind.

"Pick up any Japanese?"

"I've got a Japanese wife and kid."

"Katya is Polish."

"I know. She told me. She's a nice lady."

"She's a pretty good wife."

He helped Katya into the car and then pushed the chair back into the hospital. I liked the porters better than the doctors here.

When she saw Katya entering the apartment with me, Madame Fifi's rapture lasted a full, frenzied and boisterous five minutes. This drew the attention of the person living next door.

He approached us with purpose. "The rules of the condominium corporation stipulate that, unless it is a service animal, there are no pets allowed in this building. Is that a service animal?"

"Isn't she just so cute though?" I said. "We're checking out today."

"Is that a service animal?"

I said, "seizure sniffer" at the same time as Katya said, "No." Madame Fifi leapt into Katya's arms for protection. I gathered my things under the stern gaze of the condominium man while Madame Fifi wriggled with delight bestowing French kisses.

During our ride home, I said, "Did you see you got flowers from Val Papadopolis so you would buy that condo from her?"

"I wouldn't live there. We can just re-do our kitchen and stay where we are. I was thinking about it in the hospital."

"I see."

"Did Michael call you on your birthday?"

"He texted me."

"What did he say?"

"Two words. Happy birthday."

"That's all I got on my birthday," Katya said.

"You won't fucking believe what happened to me while you were in the hospital. Do you remember Dolly, the lady from my street in Scarborough who calls me on the phone?"

"Yes."

"Dolly drugged me with her sleeping pills and put me in a taxi to Scarborough where we got mugged."

"I don't fucking believe it."

"That's what actually happened. The cab driver mugged us while I was passed out and dumped us at Midland and Kingston Roads. She checked me into the Snowy Castle Motel, which was across the street. I must have walked into the motel, but I have no memory of it. When I found Dolly at her house the next day, she begged me not to call the police."

"So, no cops?"

"No."

"Are you done with her forever?"

"Probably. She's lonely and wants to be my horny godmother. I can't hate her for loving me. She's a fruitcake, but she's my fruitcake."

"No one can say that your life is boring, hon."

When we got home, Katya had to empty her colostomy bag. She had to wear an appliance, a plastic bag glued to her colostomy site and strapped to her waist, to collect faeces. It was something she did without complaining. I examined the site daily for signs of skin breakdown or infection, but she kept it clean and dry, and it was okay.

I returned to work on a Monday after being off for a week. The schedule had me in the general surgery room with Chandler. He nodded hello as he entered to do the preoperative check list. He recited the obligatory liturgy saying the patient's name and procedure out loud and asking whether anyone had any concerns.

Sara and I stopped getting ready for the case to pay attention. Standing quietly by was like standing for the national anthem or getting instructions from the referee before a sporting event. Wrong procedures on wrong patients on the wrong side of the body still occasionally happened, but this ritual certainly decreased the incidence. We each answered in turn that we had no concerns, allowing the surgeon also to be unconcerned.

"How is your wife doing?" Chandler asked as soon as the patient was asleep. "I heard you had some problems in Toronto."

"You heard right."

"You know, I normally would have done that polypectomy myself. I referred your wife on to Toronto because we were together for Val Papadopolis' case and I thought you might have second thoughts about my abilities. In any case, we would have had to see each other every day if something went wrong."

Doctors who work in teaching hospitals generally have made a better impression on their bosses than their peers during their years of specialty training in order to have been offered their positions. This usually included more sycophantic ass-kissing. These bosses would have had to follow the same pattern to get to where they were.

Academic physicians are more likely to be up to date and have access to the best, most expensive equipment. On the other hand, academic doctors have to train residents, so they do fewer procedures themselves. The surgeon who is the most adept at a procedure is likely to be the one who does the highest number of them. And there is a good chance if one goes the teaching hospital route, one's procedure will be performed by a trainee.

"I respect that. I think you made a good choice," I said. It probably was the right choice if he felt uncomfortable. Things might have turned out much better if he hadn't sent us to Toronto. My instructions would have been honoured in my home institution. "Put it out of your mind."

"Did the resident say how many cases like yours he'd done when he took your consent? If they haven't done any, they don't bring it up. If they've done one, they say, 'in my experience.' If they've done two, they say, 'time after time,' when they're telling you about the procedure."

"He didn't say." I felt a wave of affection for Chandler. "We should go out for a beer sometime. Do you like to drink?"

Chandler looked up from his work. "Do I ever. Right out of the juice box."

I told Chandler I was taking a 15-minute lunch, which he didn't object to. Surgeons would love to work through lunch because they are paid fee for service and can take their breaks during the time that cases are changed over. Chandler was of a newer generation. There was no point in objecting as the previous generation of surgeons did because, in either case, I would have gone anyway. We both knew that with the 15 minutes for my patient interview and setup, it would be closer to half an hour before we started up again.

Chandler left the O.R. and dejectedly turned toward the surgical ward. While I was walking briskly toward the cafeteria, I heard my name being called. I looked behind me and saw Jeremiah Chang, our Chinese Buddhist pediatrician. He was wearing his signature dark suit, narrow dark tie and as a concession to the current fashion, a hospital-issue Covid mask. "Are you going to lunch, Matthew?" he asked.

"Hi Jeremiah. Yes."

"I am going that way too, Matthew."

"Would you like to join me?"

"Yes, I would. You seem to have more time these days, Matthew."

"There's a new generation of less demanding surgeons taking over."

"It is good that they are becoming more understanding of your needs. You also have learned to choose the middle path between taking time for sufficient nourishment and not upsetting your surgical colleagues. The surgeons are not your enemies."

"Did you get a new cat yet, Jeremiah?" Jeremiah had suffered over the contradiction in having his aging, incontinent cat euthanized and his Buddhist opposition to killing.

"I have a dog now. Lucy was a very good cat and I felt sure her spirit would be promoted. I believe that Lucy's spirit has found a home in my dog, whom I have named Lucy. I believe it from the way she looks at me. I can't be certain of course since she cannot speak."

"So, no hard feelings over being euthanized?"

"She initially blamed me, but I believe she has forgiven me because she is able to appreciate the difficulty of our situation then."

"I'm glad, Jeremiah."

We reached the cafeteria and joined the lineup. The serving lady gave me an extra huge portion of shepherd's pie, explaining that I was a big person and that she had heard good things about my professional abilities. Jeremiah was also rewarded but only with extra vegetables.

We shared a table, sitting six feet apart and removed our Covid masks. "We'll have to coordinate our inhalations and exhalations to minimize the Covid," I said.

"Of course, working with children, I have had this illness and every other common respiratory virus," he said. "Matthew, how is Katya?"

"She's back home with me, feeling better now. She nearly died. She has a colostomy."

"I felt that this would happen."

"They disregarded my explicit instructions and let a resident do her surgery."

"You must let go of this anger, Matthew. It is a poison, like greed or ignorance. Anger can only be self-destructive. Karma will deal with these arrogant assholes who did not honour your explicit instructions."

"I wish I could believe that, Jeremiah. Are you keeping a vigilant eye on your cell phone these days?"

"Matthew, I am glad that you are taking an active role in the rehabilitation of Tyson Gruber."

"That's a stretch. Why would you say that?"

"He was sent to me by the Children's Aid Society for a psychological assessment. It is likely that he was born to an addicted mother and consequently was born addicted."

"It doesn't seem to have harmed him intellectually," I said.

"No, not that. If he is re-exposed, he is at increased risk of becoming re-addicted and re-offending."

"He says he hates drugs. I actually believe in him."

"So do I." Jeremiah said.

He hadn't eaten much of his lunch. Mine was mostly gone. I chose shepherd's pie because it slides down one's throat with less chewing than time-consuming vegetables.

When I got home, Katya was vacuuming, and the dog was whining and trying to bite the vacuum wand to save her. Madame Fifi had not yet reached enlightenment with respect to machines. Katya turned off the motor when she saw me.

"Shouldn't you be resting?" I asked.

"I'm fine. Who did you work with today?"

"I was working with Chandler. He's sorry about what happened and told me he normally would have done your procedure himself. He referred it on because you're a doctor's wife."

"I guess I should have had Chandler do it."

"Hindsight is twenty-twenty. Maybe I should have asked Isaiah. He's the most experienced endoscopy surgeon in Coventry. His cocaine habit didn't diminish that. It was probably more of a cocaine dalliance."

"They say you shouldn't cry over spilt milk."

Chapter 21

"What was that?" Katya asked.

"I changed my phone ring tone," I said.

"It sounds like the Jeopardy theme song."

"It's chilling isn't it. Anything can sound menacing in the right context."

I glanced at the phone screen, which read *Coroners' Answering Service*, and reluctantly picked up.

"Hello Doctor. Could you help us out with a call at Somerset Hospital? It's a death in their emergency department."

"That's a 50-minute drive."

"We've tried everyone else. Could you help us out?"

I had actually done an anesthesia locum in Somerset 20 years ago when our operating rooms were slow, and I was younger and hungrier. It was deep in Mennonite country and chronically short-staffed. Rural hospitals had difficulty attracting Canadian-trained doctors and often relied on foreign medical graduates.

"Okay. Give me the information."

The dispatcher gave me the decedent's name, Ezekiel Gruber, his date of birth and the number of the doctor who was calling. He thanked me and hung up.

"They've been calling you a lot lately," Katya said.

"I think the other coroner in this area must be away on holiday."

I called the Somerset Hospital number and was routed to a Dr. Gilmadi who was covering their emergency department. She told me that Ezekiel Gruber was a 57-year-old man who had come in with abdominal pain and had suffered a cardiac arrest. Gruber is a common Mennonite surname. I agreed to accept the case because he was youngish and previously healthy, and consequently the death was sudden and unexpected.

Out of respect for the dead, and not wanting to offend relatives, I changed out of my blue jeans and T-shirt into something more respectable—dark jeans and a shirt with a collar and a pocket for pens and business cards. I'm not an undertaker, so I don't go as far as putting on a black suit. Heading out onto the highway, I cruised through nondescript treeless farmland. The landscape was broken up by the occasional driveway or creek or black Mennonite buggy as I got closer to Somerset.

Arriving at the hospital, I went in through the emergency department entrance. I passed the walking wounded seated in the waiting room through to where the more seriously ill waited on stretchers. One of the nurses ushered me to the nursing station. Dr. Gilmadi was seated at a long counter working on her notes. She looked to be in her early forties, plump, stethoscope dangling around her neck. After the preliminary introductions, I sat down beside her and waited for her to tell her story.

Dr. Gilmadi told me that Mr. Gruber had come in complaining of abdominal pain and vomiting. She had sent him for an abdominal CT scan in the X-Ray Department. The technician who was doing the scan had called her to say that the patient was agitated and moving too much for good images, and could they please have the patient sedated. She had gone over to the X-Ray department and administered some intravenous sedation. When he still didn't settle, she gave him more. I asked her what she had used, and she said midazolam, then fentanyl and then ketamine.

When Mr. Gruber came out of the scanner, his condition had deteriorated and they called her back to the X-Ray department. She arrived with a nurse and a crash cart. Dr. Gilmadi assisted his breathing with bag-mask ventilation, passed an endotracheal tube, and gave intravenous fluids and vasopressors. Despite this he continued to deteriorate and arrested. A cardiac arrest was announced over the public address system, and the arrest team arrived to assist her. They were unsuccessful in reviving him.

She showed me a double-sided paper flowchart where nurses had entered all the medications and the times that they had been given. She recited the names of vasopressor drugs she had used. As the drugs had failed, and he was dead, this didn't impress me. They don't address the underlying condition. She knew the names of the drugs, but after a patient has deteriorated to the point of cardiac arrest, they almost never work.

A nurse who was at the nursing station said that although his health card said Ezekiel Gruber, they had found a drivers' licence in the decedent's wallet in the name of Mordechai Yantzi. She handed me both plastic cards.

The CT scan had revealed that Mr. Gruber or Yantzi had a perforated intestine, possibly from diverticulitis. Dr. Gilmadi's best guess was that her patient had died from septicemia secondary to the intestinal perforation. Septicemia means infection in the bloodstream. I looked through the hospital records and then went to see the decedent. Dr. Gilmadi came along with me.

The hallway outside the CT scanner was barricaded with portable screens. The floor was littered with wrappers for syringes and needles and intravenous tubing. The decedent was lying on a gurney inside the enclosure. He was dressed in a hospital gown open at the front. He was thin and dark-haired with a two-day growth of beard.

There was an endotracheal tube poking out of his mouth and defibrillation pads stuck to the front and side of his chest. I held both plastic cards up to his face.

"He looks more like a Mordechai Yantzi than an Ezekiel Gruber," I said to Dr. Gilmadi.

There was a plastic Laerdal bag, used for ventilating the lungs, discarded on the foot of the stretcher. I connected it to the endotracheal tube and squeezed while listening with a stethoscope over his chest. There were breath sounds on both sides as the chest rose and fell.

"The tube seems to be in the right place," I said.

Dr. Gilmadi looked pleased. Unskilled operators have been known to accidentally place the endotracheal tube in the esophagus. This is a lethal mistake.

There wasn't too much else to find on examining the decedent. His pupils were dilated, one was deviated. Although his face was covered in vomit, it looked familiar. He had a healed inguinal hernia scar. It was too early for the post-mortem changes of rigor or lividity to have set in.

I suspected that the doctor had given too much sedation and that that had depressed her patient's breathing. She should have used the reversal agents naloxone and flumazenil, avoiding the need to paralyze and intubate. He likely aspirated vomit into his lungs after he was paralyzed. I consoled her that she did the best she could in difficult circumstances, and we went back to the emergency department together. She went back to work and I pored over the charts, making notes for my report.

A mandatory part of my job is conveying my findings to the next of kin. I asked a nurse if the relatives were in the quiet room. She said the decedent was brought in by a son in his thirties, who had been in a hurry to leave. I had to be satisfied with his telephone number. The nurse said that he was dressed in typical Mennonite garb, so

I was lucky to get that. I decided to give him time to get home in his buggy and try calling later.

Back in my truck on the county roads, I started thinking about what I had seen on the nurses' flowcharts. The patient's oxygen saturation was rapidly deteriorating when he came out of the CT scanner. The doctor had given rocuronium, a paralyzing agent, before passing the endotracheal tube. There had been a six-minute gap in charting after the rocuronium was given.

I pulled over to the side of the road, telephoned the hospital emergency department and asked to speak directly with the nurse who had been doing the charting. I hadn't spoken with her before, and she sounded nervous. I asked her about the six-minute gap. She said they had probably been too busy to keep up with the charting. Knowing that there is a nurse dedicated to this, I didn't like her response. I asked her again why there was a gap in charting immediately after the rocuronium.

She was stuttering when she replied. She said that when the arrest team arrived, the patient's oxygen saturation had been very low, and that the anesthesiologist had acted very quickly to remove and replace the endotracheal tube that Dr. Gilmadi had inserted. The oxygen level had risen promptly to 90 percent after that. She hadn't wanted to record this event or an oxygen saturation of ten percent on the chart.

I thanked her, called the hospital switch board and asked to speak to the anesthesiologist on call. I waited on hold until he picked up. Introducing myself as a coroner and fellow anesthesiologist, I asked him what he had observed at the arrest scene. He reluctantly told me that the endotracheal tube had been esophageal and that he had removed and placed it correctly into the trachea. The patient had normal anatomy, so it wasn't difficult.

It made me angry that Dr. Gilmadi had omitted to tell me about this—in effect lied to me. Emergency physicians can't possibly be as good at airway management as anesthesiologists. They don't do it every day. I had worked as a full-time emergency doctor before training to become an anesthesiologist. Knowing that there was a specialist for everything, who was better at and could second guess anything I did, was what drove me out of the field.

I swung my car around and drove back to the hospital to make photocopies of the nurses' flowcharts to get exact times for my report. The emergency department lot looked full, so I found a parking spot near the main entrance. There was a group of Mennonite women in traditional dress in the lobby. One of them looked familiar.

"Hi Anna," I said. "How is the new baby?"

"Oh, hi Dr. Kork. She's doing very well thank you."

Another woman in the group who was cradling a baby rocked it in her arms to indicate that this was the baby in question.

"Why are you here, Anna? I hope no one is sick."

"Yes. My father-in-law died. It's very sad."

I noticed Caleb now, off in the corner with some other men, the brim of his straw hat pulled down low over his eyes. He still hadn't paid my bills.

"I need to speak with you and your husband. Please follow me back to the emergency department."

Anna, holding her sleeping baby, and Caleb sat down with me in the quiet room. Mennonite children are always amazingly quiet, even in their infancy. It was done up like a small living room with carpet and real furniture. I gently shut the sound-proof door, which sealed us off from any outside disturbance. The door also prevented people in the patient area from hearing the wails of bereaved relatives.

"I am the coroner investigating Mordechai Yantzi's death," I explained. "I'm sorry for your loss Anna and Caleb. Do you mind if I ask you a few questions?"

"Okay," Anna said.

"Can you tell me when Mordechai started feeling sick and what happened after that?"

"Mordechai was visiting relatives in Pennsylvania when he got a terrible belly ache," Anna said. "He went to the hospital there and they told him to come in and stay. He came back to Canada because it was going to cost a lot of money. Doctors are free here if you have a health card."

"The doctors here think that Albert had inflammation and infection in a small outpouching of his intestine that burst," I said. "It's called perforated diverticulitis."

They were silent.

"Did Mordechai also go by the name of Albert?" I asked.

"Albert was his English name," Anna said.

I knew now why the decedent looked familiar. The lazy-eyed drug dealer I had pushed my bike past in the park after Jackson's retirement party was Albert Yantzi. His strabismus was a product of his parents' swimming in a small gene pool.

"Did Albert bring his health card?" I asked.

"He lost it, but the hospital knows his number," Anna said.

"He should have stayed in Pennsylvania," Caleb said.

"Caleb, your half-sister Taylor put in an insurance claim for death benefits on Albert a few months ago."

"Mebbie she thought he was dead," Caleb said.

"Caleb, everyone thought he was dead," I said.

"He never said he was dead. You just thought he was because he was missing."

"Caleb, there was a dead body in his apartment."

"Yes."

"How did that get there?"

"He loaned his apartment to a friend sometimes when he went away."

"Do you know the name of the friend whose body we found?"

"He had many friends. Mebbie it was Ezekiel."

"Was Ezekiel's last name Gruber?"

"Mebbie so."

"Ezekiel Gruber already had his own apartment."

"Mebbie it wasn't him."

"Albert was using Ezekiel Gruber's health card today," I said.

They didn't respond.

"Do you know whether Albert owned a ladder?" I asked.

They were silent and then Anna said, "Caleb, Albert borrowed your long ladder two months ago." Albert was easier than Mordechai to say even for Anna.

"Hau ab!" Caleb looked angry with Anna. "Well, he brought it back too, so that's fine."

Caleb didn't realize that I understood German. He had told Anna to shut up. "Did your father use drugs?" I asked him, knowing the answer already.

"I don't know."

"Yes," Anna said.

"Caleb and Anna, there will be an autopsy, probably tomorrow, in Toronto to find out positively why Albert died. I will call you tomorrow after I know the result. Do you have a telephone number where I can reach you?"

"You can call me on my cell," Caleb said.

He drove a buggy but had a cell phone. Anna got up, cradling her baby. "Okay. We will go to visit with Mordechai now." Her dignified tone indicated that they were taking their leave of me.

They got up and went to pay their last respects to Mordechai slash Albert. I corralled the paper flowcharts, Albert's driver's licence and the stolen health card at the nursing station and asked the clerk to make photocopies for me. I needed to speak with Branko, but I wanted to do it from home. Driving back through the empty farmlands was time well spent organizing my thoughts. It didn't seem long before I arrived at the suburbs of Coventry. The drive back from a coroner call always seemed faster than the drive to it.

Chapter 22

Reaching the outskirts of Coventry was like reaching an oasis. The sun was shining and the leaves, which were turning colour, were fluttering in the breeze. The water in the canal that divided the city into rich and less fortunate was calm and pretty. The traffic was calm. There were no horse-drawn Mennonite buggies. I pulled my FJ Cruiser into our driveway and raised the garage door.

Brushing past Katya in the kitchen, I said, "Hi. Sorry. I have to make a phone call," and rushed to my study. Spreading my notes out on my desk, I tried Branko's personal cell number. He sounded like he was in his car when he answered.

"Can you talk?" I asked.

"Yes. I'm not alone. If it's police business, I'll pull over and take the call off speakerphone."

"Pull over then," I said.

After a few seconds, I heard, "Okay, what's up?"

"Guess who died today."

"I give up."

"Albert Mordechai Yantzi, the decomposed corpse with the bullet in his head."

"He died again? You mean that wasn't Albert the first time?"

"No. I was with Albert less than an hour ago at Somerset Hospital. Dead again. This time from perforated diverticulitis. He came back from Pennsylvania to get free medical care."

"He must have memorized his health insurance number. He generously left his health card at the first scene to help us ID his corpse."

"I think you will find that that corpse's real name was Ezekiel Gruber. Albert had Mr. Gruber's health card. I expect that the body was in Albert's apartment as part of an insurance fraud scheme. Either Albert or Caleb or both of them together could have done the killing. They both stood to benefit. Caleb might still be in the emergency department now, grieving his father. If you hurry, you can pick him up."

"I'll bring him in tomorrow for questioning."

"He might be in Pennsylvania by tomorrow."

"Flight would be a good indicator of guilt. I've had him under intermittent surveillance. I'll have somebody keep an eye on his house overnight."

"They'll be noticed on the treeless landscape in Mennonite country."

"Good. He'll know not to run. It's my day with my kids today, Matt. Caleb's not going anywhere."

"Why not?"

"He has to stay to collect on Albert's life insurance policy, for one."

"True… The DNA sample from the decomposed body in Albert's apartment should show paternity to Ezekiel Gruber's son Tyson if we get a DNA sample from him. That would provide positive ID."

"Can you organize that?"

"Sure."

The coroner's office would have to spring for the expense of not one, but two, DNA tests after all.

"Okay. I've been horseback riding and axe throwing today," Branko said. "I still have to escape from an escape room, do dinner and go laser bowling."

"You better get going then."

The autopsy on the real Albert Yantzi was done the next day. Ron Rasmussen called me mid-morning with the preliminary report. He said that Albert's bowel had perforated as suspected, but not from diverticulitis. It had obstructed after becoming entangled in a large piece of polypropylene mesh in the right inguinal area. Ron hadn't been able to find hernia mesh in the first Albert Yantzi autopsy. This should have been a clue for us as to the mistaken identity.

The pathologist reported that a trapped segment of bowel had necrosed and the obstruction had caused this to distend and perforate. It had also caused the stomach to be full of backed-up feculent material. Albert had regurgitated and aspirated these stomach contents into his lungs. The aspiration could have happened any time in the immediate pre-mortem period, but not earlier, because the lungs showed no inflammation.

I knew that Dr. Gilmadi had been struggling, trying to get the endotracheal tube into the right throat hole. She was performing bag-mask ventilation between intubation attempts. The aspiration had happened during the six-minute gap that the endotracheal tube had been in and out of his esophagus, and the trachea, or windpipe, was not protected from the liquid poop welling up in his throat.

Ron said that he could only report on his findings as they were. Having not been at the scene and having never managed an airway, he wouldn't appreciate that the intubation should have been easy and that the death was avoidable. Coroners aren't supposed to be judgemental. Being an anesthesiologist, I couldn't help but be.

Having two decedents, I had two phone calls to make. I never like to be the first to inform the next of kin of a death. I interview them at the scene if they are present, but otherwise wait until the next day when police have already done the notification. It allows me to express simple condolences and then proceed without waiting for the news to be absorbed and the heart-rending weeping to abate.

My first call was to Ezekiel Gruber's next of kin, Tyson. Sean Feeney had given me his cell number. Tyson answered on the first ring.

"Hi Tyson. It's Dr. Matthew Kork."

"Hello. Are you ready to play some more golf?"

"No. Did the police get in touch with you yesterday about your father?"

"Yes. I know he's dead."

"I'm sorry about your loss. I'm calling because I'm the coroner investigating your father's death. Do you have a moment to talk?"

"Yes."

"I'm not sure what the police have already told you. Your father likely died five months ago. He was cremated as Albert Yantzi, whose apartment he was found in.

"Yes, I know."

"Tyson, did you ever meet a man named Albert or Mordechai Yantzi through your father?"

"No. I don't know him."

"He was slim, dark haired and one of his eyes was turned outward."

"Sorry. Doesn't ring a bell."

"Did your father ever talk about harming himself or see a psychiatrist?"

"No. He harmed himself with drugs, but he never said he wanted to kill himself."

"Would you be able to come for a DNA test to prove that the body in that apartment was your dad? I'm 99 per cent sure that it was. It just involves taking a swab from the inside of your cheek."

"Okay."

"This mistake in identification was planned by Albert Yantzi who left his own identification with your father's body. Mr. Yantzi is also dead. We will never know all the facts for sure, but I suspect that he was responsible for your father's death."

"The police told me he was shot in the head."

"Yes. I'm sorry."

"My father was a drug dealer. He was killed by a drug addict."

"Tyson, was your father right or left-handed?"

"He was definitely right-handed. He would sometimes have needle marks on his left arm if he was sampling product."

I was impressed by his dispassionate, matter-of-fact tone.

"Once again. I'm sorry for your loss. How are things going in your new foster home?"

"The people seem nice. They're getting paid to let me stay."

"Other than you, did your father have any other adult relatives?"

"Nobody I keep in touch with. He had friends at Gleeson Court."

"I hope it works out for you there in your new place."

"Thanks."

I gave Tyson instructions on where to go to give the DNA sample. It just involved going to the Coventry Hospital laboratory where they would take the specimen and arrange for it to be shipped to the Centre of Forensic Sciences in Toronto. I emailed the Toronto lab to let them know that the specimen was coming and asked them what the test costs.

My second call was to Caleb Yantzi. It was hard to know which Mennonites would have phones, drive cars or have health insurance. Traditional dress wasn't always predictive. Depending on the congregation they belonged to, they could have any one of those things and not the other. Under no circumstances were Old Order Mennonites ever allowed television or radio. Caleb promptly answered his cell phone when I called.

I told him that the autopsy showed that Albert's bowel had perforated because it had obstructed after becoming entangled in a large piece of polypropylene mesh that was used to repair a right inguinal hernia. I told him how to obtain a copy of the coroner's report by applying in writing to the Regional Supervising Coroner and did he have any questions?

Caleb absorbed the information in his usual taciturn manner. He wondered why anyone would put mesh into a hernia if this could happen. I told him it was a standard practice and the benefits likely outweighed the risks. Caleb wanted to know whether I would finally complete the life insurance policy claim form. That was it.

I don't normally call more than one next of kin. I make the relatives decide amongst themselves who that is and assign that person to inform the others. Having spoken with Caleb, my duty was theoretically done. Because I had originally communicated with Taylor, I felt obligated to call her as well. She was still listed as Albert's official next of kin. She was back in Toronto when I reached her.

"When I first contacted you about your father, it wasn't your father who had died," I told her. "He died yesterday. The cause of your father's death was that a section of his bowel died and started to leak and spread infection. The bowel became tangled in mesh that was used to repair a hernia years before. The manner of death was natural." Surgical complications are considered acts of God and therefore natural.

"I understand."

"The pathologist is finished with your father's body and is ready to release it."

"Do you want me to take care of the funeral home arrangements or do you want Caleb to do it?"

"You can decide between yourselves. Your father's body is at the Forensic Services Complex in Toronto. You'll have to choose a funeral home to look after picking him up. There is no charge to you for the transport or for the autopsy. The funeral home will want to know whether you want a burial or cremation."

"Okay. I'll take care of it."

"Taylor, after the first time I contacted you, did Caleb call you to tell you about the life insurance policy?"

"Yes."

"So, you didn't really find the policy in his apartment?"

"Caleb told me where to look in the apartment."

"Taylor, is Oliver your nephew?"

"Yes."

"I had him as a patient recently."

"He's a really nice little boy. Parker didn't want Albert to have anything to do with him. She told me my father wanted to see him sometimes but he was mostly drunk or high so she wouldn't allow it. He threatened to sue her, but he never did. Please don't tell Parker that I was telling you about it."

"I don't expect to see her again."

"Okay."

"Parker was the one who reported your father's death to police. She had gone to his apartment."

"She hadn't seen him in a long time. They had some things to talk over."

"Were they still doing drugs together?"

"She says they weren't."

I didn't discuss my concerns around the esophageal intubation with Taylor or Caleb. Who would it have helped if I had told them directly that Dr. Gilmadi was responsible for their father's death. What was done was done.

Dr. Gilmadi had done her best. As an emergency physician, she had to be a "Jill of all trades," and consequently a master of none. She was not an expert in airway management. They would see it if they knew how to read between the lines of my report. They probably wouldn't of course. A medico-legal lawyer certainly would.

After telling Taylor I didn't intend to speak with Parker again, I abruptly changed my mind. There was a point I wanted to clarify with her. I went through my billing records for Oliver Riordan to find Parker's telephone number and dialled it.

"May I speak with Parker Riordan please."

"This is Parker."

"Parker, sorry for calling so late. This is Dr. Matthew Kork. We met when I gave Oliver's anesthetic. I'm also the coroner investigating the death of Albert Yantzi."

"Yes. Hello."

"I was hoping you could clear up a question I have about Albert. You were the one who reported his death to police, is that correct?"

"Yes, but we weren't together anymore."

"Why did you go to his apartment that day?"

"I needed his signature to take Oliver across the border to my parents' condo in Florida. It was the second time I'd been there to ask him for that. It turned out we couldn't have gone anyway after Oliver got sick, so I shouldn't have even bothered."

"Parker, your friend Piper intimated to me that Albert accidentally shot a man named Ezekiel Gruber in the head in his apartment. How would she have known that? Were you in touch with Albert after he disappeared?"

"She wouldn't have told you that."

"She told me hypothetically at a course I was teaching. I'd like to know whether it's true."

"How would I know?"

"Were you in touch with Albert after he disappeared?"

There was a long pause before she answered. "Are you recording this call?"

"No. I promise you that I'm not."

"I guess it doesn't matter now he's dead. He called me about four months ago. He said he had had to disappear because a guy in his apartment had accidentally shot himself in the head. The guy saw Albert's rifle hanging on the wall and wanted to try it. Albert wanted to know whether the body had been discovered yet, and to hear how Oliver was doing."

"He called you to ask you about the body?"

"He said Caleb needed to know for insurance reasons. If he wanted to be a good father, he should have called when Oliver was in the hospital. I guess he didn't know. Since he was a liar, what he said about the rifle was probably a lie."

"I'm sorry for your loss, Parker. You had a complicated relationship with Albert. He was Oliver's father."

"I don't miss him. I don't miss his drugs. Since I had Oliver, I don't do drugs anymore, that much."

"How is Oliver feeling?"

"He's a little sick but mostly all better. Thank you."

"This may seem like an odd question. Was Albert left or right-handed?"

"Left, like Oliver."

"Thanks for speaking with me, Parker."

Albert was left-handed. Ezekiel Gruber was right-handed. It was just perverse curiosity that made me ask.

Chapter 23

The DNA tests on samples from Ezekiel and Tyson Gruber came back three weeks later with a finding of 99% probability of paternity. The lab didn't answer my question as to how much this testing cost. With socialized medicine nobody knows the price of anything. An internet search told me that private companies charge $250 for paternity testing. I feel like that should have been affordable.

Despite our missteps, we were close to a resolution of the Albert Yantzi apartment death case. I texted Branko to call me when he was next on duty. I wanted to get my facts straight before calling Richard Tull again. *Strangers in the Night* played from the speaker and Coventry Police appeared on the call display of my phone that evening.

"Hey Matt. What's up?"

"Hi Branko. Thanks for calling. I have DNA confirmation now that the body in Albert Yantzi's apartment was Tyson Gruber's father."

"Okay, thanks."

"What did you find out about Ezekiel Gruber?" I asked.

"Albert was clean, but Ezekiel did have a criminal record. He was a successful ganjapreneur until pot was legalized. After that, he diversified into dealing narcotics and designer benzos."

"The toxicology report on him identified hydromorphone."

"These guys used to deal Oxycontin—Oxies. It's mostly hydromorphone now, diverted from addiction treatment sites, because they can cook it. Oxycontin can't be cooked and injected anymore. Gruber was probably making a delivery to Albert, and the two of them were sampling some product. Albert shot him, likely for drugs and cash. Leaving his own ID at the scene suggests he was also staging his own murder or suicide. If he was staging a suicide for insurance money, he can't have read the policy through to the end."

"Strict Mennonites don't have life insurance," I said. "God is their insurance."

"Albert wouldn't fit the description of strict Mennonite. He and Caleb couldn't wait for God to pay out."

"Was Caleb involved?"

"All he will admit to is lending his father a ladder," Branko said. "Albert would have needed it to climb down from his balcony after shooting Gruber. That's how the flies got in. I think he wanted to leave the body behind a locked door so he would have time to flee the country."

"He could have locked the door with his key."

"He didn't want to be seen by neighbours or on security cameras. The ladder shows premeditation."

I'd forgotten about the video camera in the apartment lobby. "Albert or Caleb didn't show up on camera, did they?"

"It was only there as a deterrent. The owner of the building didn't want to pay for monitoring."

"Well, couldn't you charge Caleb with conspiracy?" I felt like he must be guilty of something.

"We could try, but we don't have any proof that they conspired. We can't place him at the scene. The partial palm print on the rifle identifies Albert, not Caleb. Of course, we don't know the age of the print, and since it was Albert's rifle, the print could have been put there before the killing. Or Caleb could have worn gloves. If you can't tell us what day Gruber died, we can't expect Caleb to account for every minute of every day for three weeks."

"I saw Caleb and his father arguing in the park the night of Jackson's retirement."

"What did they say?"

"One of them said to call in the ladder, I guess to police. The other one said, 'Fuck you and stick to the plan.' Gruber would already have been dead then."

Madame Fifi didn't like the f-word and started barking. I closed the door to my study.

"That's probably not enough. Could you positively identify Caleb? It was dark. Was he wearing Mennonite clothes?"

"No, and I don't think so," I said.

"I'll run it past the crown attorney."

"Caleb and Albert are responsible for two deaths if you also count Sindler Collins. Couldn't you take Caleb downtown and beat a confession out of him?"

"We did bring him in. He didn't say anything incriminating."

"That's because he barely speaks."

"Is that your dog barking in the background?"

"Yes. That's Madame Fifi. Did you ask him why his father needed the ladder?"

"He didn't know. How did you pick that name, Madame Fifi?"

"In the morning when she's hungry, she barks, 'Oeuf! Oeuf!' In the evening, 'Boeuf! Boeuf!' "

"Funny. If we weren't East European brothers from different mothers, I would say you were a cunning linguistic show-off," Branko said accusingly.

"Okay, I'm going to sign off on it as a homicide, as long as Richard Tull agrees."

"Okay. Let me know. That will put more pressure on us to name a perpetrator when it makes the news."

I was ready to call Richard Tull to discuss the latest developments. He was generally available on his cell phone during office hours and, if not, he was good about calling back. When my call went to voicemail, I left the contents of Ezekiel Gruber's file open on my desktop, made a cup of coffee and stayed close to my phone. Richard called back half an hour later.

"Sorry Matt. I was in a meeting. What's up?"

"Do you remember the case of Ezekiel Gruber who was found decomposed in his apartment with a bullet in his head from five months ago?"

"Yes. We had a case conference with the pathologist. Let me open the file online."

I waited a minute while he opened and scanned my preliminary report, which I had updated to include the information about the decedent's revised identity.

"Do we have the DNA test result back yet proving paternity to this boy Tyson Gruber?"

"Yes. It's just come back. It should be there."

"Okay. What did you want to talk about?"

"My investigation is complete. I favour calling the manner of death homicide. Ezekiel Gruber was shot in the head in Albert Yantzi's apartment. The rifle looked like it was placed by the side of the body. Albert was a user. Gruber was a dealer. Albert Yantzi had motive, opportunity and had borrowed ladder from his son. The front door was locked, but the balcony door was not. I believe Albert pulled the trigger and climbed down the ladder at night from his balcony. His son Caleb was supposed to collect on a new life insurance policy. I think they chose Gruber because Gruber resembled Albert physically, and for cash and drugs."

"It's ultimately up to the police to determine criminality. What's their opinion?"

"The investigating officer is Detective Branko Markovic. He's leaning toward calling it murder although he has no one to charge with the crime."

"The evidence sounds circumstantial."

"Isn't the coroner's verdict based on the balance of probabilities? Can I enter my verdict as homicide on my final report?"

"It's a little different with a homicide verdict if it could lead to a criminal charge. Let me speak to Detective Marcovic personally. Give me his contact information."

We left it at that. During the 1990's, the mantra for coroners was *think dirty*. In that era, based on findings made by one now-discredited, pediatric forensic pathologist, coroners' verdicts of homicide were rendered for 20 children in Ontario. The parents were subsequently wrongfully convicted of killing their own children. Since then, Regional Supervisors have become more cautious. The new mantra is *think*.

I had another retirement party to attend that evening. Katya didn't feel ready to socialize yet, but I was obligated to go. It was for the oldest member of the anesthesia department, Casper Stills, making me the new oldest member. The party was in a local craft brewery. The parking lot was full when I arrived, so I parked on the grassy verge beside it.

It looked like there were about a hundred people inside, about half of whom were retired nurses. Either they really liked Casper, or they enjoyed each other's company or their lives were meaningless and empty after they stopped working. Everyone had a craft beer in their hand. I talked to the nurses in the beer lineup and once I was served went over to Casper to shake hands.

"How did you know it was time?" I asked him.

"When the pile of chips you've stacked up is high, but not about to fall over," he said.

"That might describe me," I said.

"When you practice anesthesia, there is a constant small risk of disaster. A boxer and a gambler have to know when to quit. You have to know when to cash out and walk away with your winnings."

"So, it's not that you were stressed out or felt dangerous, had something else you would rather be doing or had enough money?"

"It was all four. I have enough money. The average life expectancy for a Canadian male is 78. That means I have ten years left to live. There are no luggage racks on hearses."

"I don't know whether I would know what to do with myself if I retired."

"You'll get there and you'll figure it out," Casper said.

Our conversation was interrupted for some speeches—nurses relating anecdotes from the front lines. Casper got up and said that he wouldn't miss getting called out from a dead sleep in the middle of the night to rush to the hospital to pull victory from the jaws of defeat. He might miss some of the people.

I noticed Sara from across the room. Everyone else must have too. She was wearing a form-fitting dress of a shiny, knit material. Her figure was a tight hourglass. She made her way through the crowd toward me. Her eyes were large and luminous green, magnified by eyeliner and mascara. The outer line of her lipstick was precisely perfect. She looked great.

"Hi Matt. How are you?" She was standing in front of me holding a glass of wine. She was too perfect to hug out a greeting.

"Pretty good. You look amazing."

"Thanks. There's a good turnout tonight."

"There are even some surgeons. I don't think many will show up for my retirement. I'm going to be embarrassed tonight when I don't remember the name of a nurse I haven't seen in a few years."

"How is your wife, Matt? You were saying she's back home again."

"Yes. She's much better, thanks."

"I'm glad she's okay. Couldn't she come tonight?"

"No. She doesn't feel quite up to it yet. She might be self-conscious about her colostomy."

"Do you think what happened was anyone's fault?"

"I think they let an inexperienced, sleep-deprived resident do the procedure as part of his training." I heard the anger in my own voice.

"Are you thinking of suing?"

"No."

"They ignored the rule that if a complication is going to happen, it will happen to a nurse or a doctor or a doctor's wife."

"Or a lawyer or a lawyer's wife," I said.

"Everyone hates lawyers, until you need one. My ex-husband was a lawyer." I hadn't known she was divorced.

"How was the experience of being part of the legal community?"

"A lot of them are shysters." She took a sip from her wine glass.

"Are you talking about your husband? Did he hide assets from you?"

"No, not that. You have to be a performer to be a good trial lawyer. My ex was always performing for the crowd. It was hard to know when he was sincere."

"Did he try to pump you for information about mistakes at the hospital?"

"No. He never sank that low," Sara said.

"Did he lie to you?"

"Sure. Amongst other things."

"Do you mean extra-marital affairs?"

"Yes, but that's water under the bridge." The noise in the room was ramping up. She edged closer to hear me speak, and I noticed her perfume. I resisted the impulse to touch her. We were friends. The experience was pleasant, but not sexual.

Sara swirled her nearly empty wine glass side to side contemplatively. "What happens when there is a medical error and the person actually dies and you're the coroner? Do you tell the family the truth of what happened?"

"Yes. I'm not allowed to tell anyone else. If I don't think that anything could be changed to prevent a similar thing happening in the future, I don't tell them directly. It would only make them feel bad. If they request a copy of the coroner's report, it's there, although in diplomatic language. They might not be able to decipher it unless they get an expert or a lawyer. I don't help lawyers rake the muck."

I had become acclimatized to Sara's perfume and didn't notice it as strongly.

"How did you and Katya meet?" she asked.

"She was staring and smiling at me, so I went over and kissed her."

Sara looked surprised. "How did that go?"

"Well, I thought. It was just a peck. She was still smiling afterward."

"That is such a beautiful story. I should try that. Tell Katya, all the best," Sara said.

"Thanks Sara. I will."

"You're a good husband, Matt."

"Thanks."

She drifted away toward Chandler.

At the end of the evening, the retired nurses lined up at the exit to tell Casper not to go back to work no matter how much anyone begged. I thought he was still safe to work, but maybe they knew something that nobody was openly talking about. Alternatively, maybe the administration had been begging the nurses, who had retired early due to Covid, to return and they were looking to make a common front.

Chapter 24

Katya had the morning newspaper spread out on the kitchen table. I was scrolling through the news and weather on my phone. It was another scene of domestic bliss. I love the morning because the day is still high with promise.

"Sleep well?" I asked.

"No. Want to hear my dream?" Katya asked.

"Of course, hon."

"I dreamt I had to find a husband. I was out with my sister, competing with her, trying to find a husband—but the men were only interested in her."

"You know you're identical twins, right?"

"That didn't seem to matter."

"I thought you and your friends had moved on. All of your clubs exclude husbands. Why would you want another one?"

"I don't know. I just wanted one."

"If you lived with a woman, you would have similar interests and be on the same wavelength emotionally." I opened the next article on the BBC news app.

Katya fell silent. Glancing up from my phone, I saw that she was giving me a soul-searching look. I guess I crave normalcy and routine. I was overjoyed to have her back home.

She said, "I still get a little thrill when you crawl into bed with me."

I met her gaze. "You know, I love you now more than ever."

"Because you were closer to losing me?"

"No. I don't know why."

"I love you just as much as I always did," she said.

"Ah. That's sweet."

"I wasn't holding any love back."

"I love you one more than whatever you say."

"The colostomy doesn't bother you?" Her eyes were glassy.

"No."

I took Katya in my arms and held her longer than a comfortable five seconds. I gave her a peck on the cheek and then went about the business of making my breakfast, while she went about the business of doing the newspaper crossword puzzle.

There are times when I wonder what my life would have been like if my parents had made decisions affecting my life, or I had made any one of a thousand decisions, slightly differently, resulting in my never meeting Katya. Would I have been as happy having married someone else, having different children, having different friends.

There is a theory that every decision between two alternatives that you make spawns two different universes, which play out with the ramifications of that decision. The alternate lives might be better or might indeed be worse. The question has no answer. I only know that the life that I have is good.

Ezekiel Gruber's case was wrapped up as follows. After speaking with Branko, Richard Tull called me back to suggest we label his manner of death as undetermined. Being an obedient soldier, this is what I did. Undetermined didn't close any doors and the police could still continue to investigate the case as a homicide. Apparently, we couldn't categorically rule out suicide.

Of course, it isn't logical that Ezekiel Gruber would shoot himself in the head in Albert's apartment with Albert's rifle. I argued that Gruber was shot in the left ear. Suicides don't shoot themselves in the eye or ear. They don't want to see or hear the shot coming. Gruber was right-handed, as is 90 per cent of the population. If he did commit suicide, he would have engaged the trigger with his right hand, and shot himself in the right ear. Richard said that if he engaged the trigger with his foot, either side was possible.

I don't one hundred per cent know whether Albert and Caleb were committing a murder or staging a suicide. Maybe they didn't care either way. They weren't trying to hide the fact that Gruber had been shot in the head. If Albert was identified as a murder victim, they could collect on the insurance. If they were staging a suicide, they were too stupid to know that insurance companies don't pay for suicides. My theory is that they found out suicides weren't covered after the killing, the night I saw them arguing in the park.

When Richard called me, I asked him whether he would agree to a letter to Somerset Hospital requesting a Quality of Care Review for Albert Yantzi. I couldn't just completely sweep what had happened under the carpet. Richard agreed, and I composed the letter laying out the issues of concern, which he signed and sent. This did not place the hospital administration under any obligation to act or report back. Hospitals usually complied. Doing a Quality of Care Review kept the matter confidential, because the records of a review could not be subpoenaed by a lawyer for any kind of civil action.

I heard that Dr. Gilmadi was subsequently sent for some courses to upgrade her skills. She would never of course attain the expertise of an anesthesiologist in airway management, or of an ophthalmologist in removing corneal foreign bodies, or of an orthopedic surgeon in reducing forearm fractures… The training would help a bit, but her skills would inevitably degrade again through lack of practice.

Caleb was never prosecuted for conspiracy. I know that he was involved from the way he was promoting a murder verdict to me. The only way Albert could benefit was if Caleb collected and shared the proceeds of the insurance payout with him. Justice wasn't served, but Anna Yantzi does need a father for her five children.

Going through Albert's phone, the police found a text to Tyson Gruber. It said that he had to lay low for a while and might not be able to contact Tyson. It was sent after Ezekiel Gruber had died and was signed Dad. This was the second text that Tyson thought he received from his father after he had disappeared. Albert must have sent the first one from Ezekiel's phone before discarding it. The texts ensured no one would look too hard for him.

I filled out new insurance claim forms for Taylor McGuire with natural causes as the manner of death. She sent me a thank you note and a cheque for $75. Branko told me that she and Caleb shared a death benefit of $250,000—maybe enough for a down payment on a downtown Toronto condo now that prices were declining. Branko said that Taylor threw a few bucks to Oliver, Parker's son. He wasn't named as a beneficiary, but Parker and Taylor were close, and relations between them might otherwise have become strained when Taylor's standard of living suddenly improved.

It's hard to believe that Taylor was in on Albert and Caleb's original scheme to defraud the insurance company. She seemed too forthright and sweet. She had a beautiful face, but not a devious one. I think that Albert was trying to make amends with her by naming her as a beneficiary. I also believe that Parker at some stage told Taylor that her father wasn't really dead. That does make her a little devious.

Taylor had Albert Yantzi's remains shipped to Peterborough for disposal by alkaline hydrolysis. There are only four funeral homes in the province doing this procedure. His body was dissolved in a metal cannister using strong alkali, heat and pressure over three hours. The liquid went into the municipal waste water system.

Taylor didn't reciprocate her father's post-mortem affection. She had him cremated the first time he died. This time, she rapidly and permanently erased any physical traces of him from existence. If she had refused to claim the body, it would eventually have been incinerated at government expense, and she could have saved herself several thousand dollars.

Two weeks after completing the insurance claim forms, I received payment for anesthesiology services from Anna and Caleb Yantzi. The cheque came in a small square envelope accompanied by a close-up picture of a baby. On the back of the photo, carefully printed in a woman's handwriting, were the words: Abigail Naamah Yantzi, born May 18, 7 lbs. 9 oz, 20″ long, thankful parents: Caleb & Anna. I still have the picture. The baby looked that adorable.

There was still one loose end. Sean Feeney told me that Tyson Gruber had left school. He had only been in foster care for a few months. He left as soon as he turned 16. He was working a factory job and living with his girlfriend on social assistance.

I called Tyson, as a friend, to catch up with what was going on in his life. For some reason, I seemed to really care about that. He answered on the second ring.

"Hey Dr. Kork. It's good to hear from you. How did my DNA test turn out?"

"It showed that Ezekiel Gruber died in that apartment. It was your father. It confirmed what we basically already knew."

"Thanks for telling me. You said it was 99 per cent sure."

"Your father didn't send the texts you received after he disappeared. One of them was on Albert Yantzi's phone. He was impersonating your dad."

"The police told me."

"I also called to find out how you're doing, Tyson."

"Oh, I'm good. I'm working on the line at the Crossman stamping plant. Good steady income."

"Tyson, what happened to your dream of becoming an electrician?" I was disappointed that I had invested an evening tutoring him, the fruit of which would never be put to good use.

"Yeah. I had to quit high school. Going to have another mouth to feed soon. Got a baby on the way."

"Congratulations."

"Never mind, Dr. Kork. I'm still going to do that electrical apprenticeship. I enrolled in night school to get my high school diploma. I got an A on the assignment you helped me with."

"How did you do in math?"

"C plus. I'm proud of that because I failed my first semester."

"Tyson, at least you know that your father didn't desert you. That's something positive to remember him by."

"He was a good father in many ways. I used to like going out on jobs with him. He was good at his work. The rain will come and wash all this shit away." Tyson was wise beyond his years. "I put a cheque in the mail to you for a hundred bucks yesterday."

"What for?"

"Guys in my shop class put a roofer's nail in the tread of your SUV tire when your wife drove it to school. I recognized it outside my apartment the day I got arrested and then again when we had dinner at Mr. Feeney's house. It's a pretty unique vehicle."

"Thanks for telling me."

"I didn't know it was your truck. We did it because it was in the teachers' lot and the nail sat nicely in that aggressive tread. I'm sorry."

"Apology accepted. Good luck, Tyson."

"Thanks. You may think that it's just talk. Call me in a few years. I'll be in my apprenticeship."

I think he really will.

IF YOU ENJOYED THIS BOOK and would like to receive notification when the next in series becomes available, please go to www.petertinits.com and fill out the contact form. Click the Free Content tab and scroll to read previews of works in progress.

Please also leave a review on Amazon and/or GoodReads.

MORE BOOKS by Peter Tinits

A CAUSE and MANNER: A sleep-deprived anesthesiologist consults his friends on dealing severely with his wife's lover—first-in-series Matthias Kork novel, published in 2020.

MILLENNIUM LAMENT: Rupi Kaur for your father—a collection of darkly humorous, illustrated poetry, published in 2022.

Manufactured by Amazon.ca
Bolton, ON

35485434R00120